# INTO THE THINNEST OF AIR

# INTO THE THINNEST OF AIR

*An Ishmael Jones mystery*

# Simon R. Green

This first world edition published 2017
in Great Britain and the USA by
SEVERN HOUSE PUBLISHERS LTD of
Eardley House, 4 Uxbridge Street, London W8 7SY.
Trade paperback edition first published
in Great Britain and the USA 2018 by
SEVERN HOUSE PUBLISHERS LTD

British Library Cataloguing in Publication Data
A CIP catalogue record for this title is available from the British Library.

ISBN-13: 978-0-7278-8757-3 (cased)
ISBN-13: 978-1-84751-873-6 (trade paper)
ISBN-13: 978-1-78010-935-0 (e-book)

*All Severn House titles are printed on acid-free paper.*

Severn House Publishers support the Forest Stewardship Council™ [FSC™],
the leading international forest certification organisation.
All our titles that are printed on FSC certified paper carry the FSC logo.

Typeset by Palimpsest Book Production Ltd.,
Falkirk, Stirlingshire, Scotland.
Printed and bound in Great Britain by
TJ International, Padstow, Cornwall.

# Myths Ancient and Modern

ANCIENT

B ack in Victorian times a certain Elliot Tyrone ran a very popular inn, the Castle. It was set just outside the small Cornish community of Black Rock Towen, not far from the coast. A well-liked and eminently respectable local man, Tyrone had been the innkeeper for more than twelve years, providing good food and drink for the townspeople with the help of his wife and two teenage daughters. And most of all, everyone looked forward to Tyrone's Christmas dinners – a special treat on that most festive of holidays. But one particular Christmas, in 1886, something happened.

Half the town knew someone attending the evening meal at the Castle that Christmas. But as the hour grew later and none of the guests returned home, their families became worried. They emerged from their houses to gather in the town square and discussed the matter with increasing concern. Finally, a deputation of the bravest souls marched through the freezing weather, up the long road to the inn.

When they arrived, lights were blazing from every window but there wasn't a sound to be heard. No songs, no revelry, no conversation. The front door was standing open, spilling bright light out into the night. The townspeople went inside, and found their missing relatives still sitting at their Christmas dinner. Up and down the long table they sat slumped in their chairs, eyes wide and staring, some with their mouths still stretched in silent screams. All of them quite dead.

The townspeople found Elliot Tyrone in his kitchen, sitting on a chair, staring at nothing. There was no trace of his wife or daughters anywhere. When questioned, Tyrone freely confessed that he had poisoned the food in his special

Christmas dinner and watched his guests die. When asked why, he said 'The Voices. The Voices told me to.' And that was all he had to say. The townspeople dragged him outside and hanged him from a nearby tree.

The Castle passed through many owners after that. But it was never as popular again.

## MODERN

In 1963 an alien starship fell from the skies and crashed in an English field. All the crew but one died in the impact. The ship held together just long enough for its transformation machines to remake the sole survivor into a human being, right down to his DNA, so he could survive without being noticed until help came. But the machines had been damaged in the crash. And they wiped all of the survivor's previous memories: of who and what he was before he was human. The newly-made man stumbled away from the crash site, dazed and confused.

## NOW

When I finally came to myself after the crash, I was a long way away. I couldn't even remember where the ship had crashed.

I have spent more than fifty years living among humanity, learning how to be human. I don't remember anything else, and I don't ever want to be anything else. I haven't aged a day in all that time. So I have to keep moving, and moving on. These days I work for the mysterious secret group known as the Organization; on the cases they send me, protecting humanity from all manner of otherworldly threats. And in return they keep me safe and hidden from the overinquisitive eyes of this modern world.

*Call me Ishmael. Ishmael Jones.*

# ONE
## A Perfectly Normal Couple

've spent most of my life working and living on my own. Not by choice, it's just safer that way. For me, and for the occasional people who drift in and out of my unusual life. Because I'm not normal, I can never have a normal life with anyone; and because I don't age, it isn't fair to tie my life to people who do. And yet, despite all my experience and better instincts, I'm no longer alone. Penny Belcourt has become my partner in crimes, and my fellow solver of mysteries. We fell in love. For better or worse. Because, after all, I'm only human.

I was spending the evening at Penny's London apartment when I first heard about Elliot Tyrone and the Castle Inn. Most of the time I live in small hotels and boarding houses. The kind of places where, as long as I pay in cash, people can be relied on not to remember my name or face. In today's surveillance-crazy world, it's not easy staying off the grid and under the radar. But I try to spend as much time with Penny as I can without putting either of us at risk.

Penny's place lies right in the heart of London's most fashionable area. Where more than one bedroom and room to swing a medium-sized cat can cost you a sizeable portion of the national debt. Penny inherited the apartment from her father, and decorated it to suit her personality: loud and colourful. The first time I walked through the door I was almost blinded by the shocking-pink carpets, the wall panels in peacock blue and Imperial Chinese yellow, and the assorted technicolour cushions. With its sturdy furniture, packed book-shelves, assorted glass sculptures and a 1920s-style telephone, so she always knows where it is, the apartment has always seemed comfortable and inviting to me. Or perhaps I just feel that way because Penny lives there.

That evening we were snuggled together on the sofa, watching some documentary about wildlife in the Scottish Highlands. Scenery porn, mostly. A glamorous presence even when relaxing at home in a baggy sweater and faded jeans, Penny has a pretty face with a strong bone structure, a wide smile, dark flashing eyes, and a mass of dark hair piled up on top of her head. Add to that a trim figure and more nervous energy than is good for her, and it means I never have to worry whether my partner can keep up with me.

Whereas I am . . . quietly anonymous. I've put a lot of time and effort into learning how to be just another face in the crowd, so I can move unnoticed in the world.

Whenever Penny and I work together, it's my job to spot the things that most people wouldn't notice; and it's her job to keep me honest, and human. We work well together, solving mysteries, identifying murderers . . . And, on occasion, dealing firmly with the odd monster.

'Have you ever been to Cornwall?' Penny said lazily.

'Not officially,' I said.

She turned her head, to give me plenty of time to know a disapproving look was on its way.

'You know, you don't have to keep secrets from me . . .'

'Not everything I know is mine to tell.'

She sniffed loudly, and went back to watching the television. I looked at her thoughtfully. She had something on her mind. I could tell.

'The scenery is lovely,' said Penny.

'It is.'

'It's good to get away,' said Penny. 'I've been thinking . . .'

'Oh, that's always dangerous,' I said.

She punched me, companionably, in the arm. 'The other day I received an invitation to attend the grand reopening of an old Cornish inn. Tyrone's Castle, just outside Black Rock Towen.'

I raised an eyebrow. 'Well, that name doesn't sound at all ominous. Why have you been invited, exactly?'

Penny shrugged. 'The people who've taken over the inn are old friends of my father, from way back when. Albert and Olivia Calvert. I think they really wanted to invite my father;

but after they found out that he'd died recently, they very kindly extended the invitation to me. They sound quite keen to have me there for the first meal in their brand-new restaurant.'

'Do you know the Calverts yourself?'

'Barely. They used to visit my father at Belcourt Manor when I was just a child. I think I only remember them because they always made a point of bringing me a big tin of Quality Street. I remember the chocolates more than I remember them.'

'Never cared much for Quality Street,' I said solemnly. 'Too many toffees. Far too much hard work involved in toffees.'

'I haven't seen the Calverts in years,' said Penny. 'They just stopped coming to see my father. I don't think I ever knew why. The invitation arrived completely out of the blue. Apparently it's to be a special pre-opening meal, for a few specially selected guests. I'm thinking of going, and I'd really like it if you were to come with me.'

I thought about it. The whole conversation, I realized, had been carefully engineered to bring us to this point.

'Why?' I said. 'You don't need me for this.'

'I always need you,' said Penny. She turned off the television, so she could give me her full attention. She knows I always find it harder to say no when she's staring straight into my eyes. 'I want both of us to go. It sounds like it could be a lot of fun.'

'It sounds like a publicity stunt to launch the new owners,' I said. 'Which means there will be local press, and photographers. You know I can't afford to be part of any publicized event.'

'Not everything is about you,' said Penny. 'What attention there is will be directed at the inn and its new owners. You'll be just another guest – my plus one. You can always hide behind me if someone points a camera in our direction.'

'Why does my going matter to you so much?'

'Because I want to be able to spend a normal weekend with you, doing normal things,' Penny said earnestly. 'We only ever go away on missions for the Organization, chasing monsters and murderers. I want us to have a nice weekend off, like any normal couple.'

'I thought you liked being Penny Belcourt, girl detective?'

'I do! Just . . . not all the time.'

I thought about it. 'You know . . . it seems to me every time we go away for the weekend somebody dies. Maybe we're a jinx. Maybe we should stay at home and never go out, and then no one would die.'

'It's just a nice weekend in a nice country inn!' said Penny. 'Nothing bad is going to happen.'

'You can't be sure of that. The kind of world we live in . . .'

'But we don't have to live in it all the time!'

I looked at her. 'Why does this matter to you so much?'

'Because I don't want everything about us to be about you and your world.'

'All right,' I said. 'If it's that important to you . . . How far is it to Black Rock Towen?'

'It's all the way down on the Cornish coast,' said Penny. 'We can take a train to the nearest good hotel, then hire a car to get us to the inn. And yes, I have looked it up. It'll make a nice break, for both of us. And the Calverts did specially ask me to be there, so I feel just a bit obligated.'

'It hasn't been that long since we finished our last case for the Organization,' I said, thinking about it. 'And they're usually pretty good about making sure their agents get some decent down time between missions. They know how easily people can burn out from too much exposure to the weird stuff. So it's unlikely we'll be interrupted.'

'Then we are going? You and me?'

'If that's what you want, we'll do it. When is this very special meal?'

Penny gave me her best devastating smile. 'Tomorrow evening.'

I sighed. 'I never stood a chance, did I?'

'No. I knew if I gave you too much time to think about it, you'd come up with loads of really good reasons why you couldn't go.'

'I suppose it would be nice to visit some place well away from the weird and the unnatural, just for a change.'

'Well . . .' said Penny.

'I think I just heard the other shoe dropping,' I said, resignedly. 'What have you found?'

Penny reached out to the side table for her laptop, balanced the machine on her lap, and fired it up. An image appeared on the screen: an old country inn standing alone against a stormy sky. The hanging sign said only 'The Castle', no mention of Tyrone. It was a squat, solid, almost brutal stone structure. Grim and grey, and not in the least inviting. It looked like it had been built to withstand whatever man or nature could throw against it and sneer at both of them. The Castle Inn was set on a clifftop, looking out over the sea, and I could almost feel the cold wind gusting in off the dark, choppy waters. The inn at the end of the world . . .

'I looked the place up, after the Calverts invited me,' Penny said cheerfully. 'And I found all kinds of weird stories not just about the inn but about the whole surrounding area.'

'Go on,' I said. 'Surprise me.'

Penny's fingers moved swiftly over the keyboard, pulling up image after image. 'Back in the eighteenth century the whole coastline was a hotbed for smugglers. They'd bring in expensive goods from France, land them on the beach, and then use the Castle as a storehouse and distribution centre. Apparently the smugglers used to spread all kinds of scary stories about ghosts and demons that walked the night at specific times, so people would know to stay indoors while the smugglers were about their business. But it only took a little digging to discover that a lot of these stories predated the smugglers, sometimes by centuries.'

'Why make up something when there are already perfectly good stories just waiting to be used?'

'Exactly!' said Penny. 'Black Rock Towen and its surroundings have a long-standing reputation as a place where people go missing. Never any clues, or even a warning. They just disappear without a trace when no one's looking. We're talking about stories that go back even before there were local records.'

'How do the locals explain these disappearances?' I said.

Penny shrugged. 'There are all kinds of theories. The locals have blamed the disappearances on everything from fairy rings to alien abductions, and ghost dogs that drag you down to Hell.' She stopped and looked at me. 'Any of this mean anything to you?'

'Not really,' I said. 'I have been to Cornwall, on occasion. Coastal areas are always rife with strange occurrences. Maybe because even the weird and uncanny like to go on holiday now and again. Is there a map showing exactly where the Castle Inn is?'

'Of course,' said Penny.

I studied the map she showed me, and nodded slowly. 'I thought so. The town is only a mile or so from the cliffs, and the inn is perched right on the edge. People could easily fall off or be blown away by the wind, and the bodies would never be found. And then, there's the smugglers. Who might well have decided it was better to make any people they encountered disappear, rather than risk being identified to the authorities. Not much mystery there.'

'There's one particular story about the Castle Inn,' said Penny. She quickly ran through the story of Elliot Tyrone, and all the people who died at his poisoned Christmas meal. 'After he was discovered, Tyrone swore that "Voices" told him to do it, which you might think was a fairly obvious defence. But he wasn't the first to talk about Voices. I've tracked down accounts of fourteen other cases where local murderers made the same claim. Some of them go way back . . .'

'Has anyone ever identified these Voices?' I said. 'Put any name to them?'

'No,' said Penny. 'But there are all sorts of interesting stories about local people being driven mad by strange voices and sounds up on the cliffs and in the local woods.'

'That's just panic, caused by wild areas and open spaces,' I said. 'A well-known phenomenon. It used to be put down to the presence of Pan, the god of wild places. It's where we get the word panic from. Anything else?'

'Elliot Tyrone was hanged from a tree right outside his inn,' said Penny. 'The tree stood there for centuries, until it was finally uprooted by a really vicious storm. But local people have sworn they've seen the tree still standing in place, outside the inn, on certain nights when the moon is full. And sometimes . . . Tyrone is still hanging from the branches!'

'Does he ever get down from the tree and take a walk around?' I said. 'Any sightings of Tyrone or any of his victims inside the inn?'

Penny looked at me. 'Don't tease me. I know you don't believe in ghosts.'

'And this is the place you want us to go to for a perfectly normal weekend?' I said.

Penny sniffed. 'I just thought you might find it interesting.'

'I do,' I said quickly. 'Do the new owners know about Tyrone?'

'Oh yes,' said Penny. 'The Calverts have their own website giving all the details. I think they plan to make a feature of it to draw in the tourists.'

'Is that why you want me to go with you?' I said. 'Because you think there might be something to these stories?'

'No!' Penny said firmly. 'I just want us to have a nice weekend away together.'

'Of course,' I said. 'We can do that.'

# TWO

## A Celebration of Murder

B lack Rock Towen turned out to be neither dark nor noticeably ominous. Evening was only starting to fall over the pleasant Cornish town as I steered the hired car through narrow and occasionally cobbled streets, past the usual quaint cottages and brightly-coloured gift shops, and handwritten signs beguiling passers-by with the promise of home-made cream teas. Typical tourist trap, really. Old-fashioned street lights were just coming on, their honey-yellow illumination shedding a pleasant glow across the scene. It was like driving through the picture on the lid of a box containing a childhood jigsaw puzzle. There weren't many people about, either because it was late or because it was late in the season and the tourists had come and gone. It all seemed very calm and very peaceful. I decided not to trust any of it, just on general principles.

I drove carefully through the small town and out the other side, then followed the single narrow road that led to the cliffs. And hopefully to Tyrone's Castle. A signpost pointed the way to the cliffs, but didn't mention the inn. The road went on for quite some time, until the town had completely disappeared in the rear-view mirror. Heavy woods crowded right up to the edge of the road on both sides, the tall thickset trees packed close together, their heavy branches leaning out over the road to form a dark green tunnel. I had to turn on the car's headlights just to see where I was going.

It felt as though we were leaving civilization behind and travelling on into a darker and more primitive place.

'We're already more than a mile outside the town,' I said to Penny. 'And there's still no sign of the inn. In fact, we're so far out of town we're probably more than half way to somewhere else. Why build an inn so far out of town in the first place?'

'Because it was built, owned and run by the local smuggling fraternity,' Penny said patiently. 'And they didn't want anyone around while they were working.'

'Then why use an inn?'

'Because it probably made for the perfect cover the rest of the time,' said Penny. 'Besides, it's traditional. I think there might even be an old law or custom, or something.'

'Still, seems like a hell of a long way for the locals to go for a drink,' I said. 'Not much in the way of transport back then, I would have thought. And this road looks like it would have made for a really spooky walk back in the dark after you've had a few.'

'On the other hand, since the owners were smugglers you can bet the Castle had the best booze for miles around.'

'Good point,' I conceded. 'Why are you scowling?'

'I really don't like this car,' said Penny. 'It's bland, characterless, and smells like something died on the back seat. Recently.'

'It's a hire car,' I said patiently. 'It goes. Be thankful for that. Of course, you could have driven us down here in one of your prized vintage cars if you hadn't written the last one off by driving it head on into a telegraph pole.'

'It was just a bump.'

'The whole front of the car was concertinaed, and the telegraph pole was left hanging in three pieces . . .'

'It wasn't my fault! The pole jumped out into the road, right in front of me.'

'Of course,' I said. 'Something must have frightened it.'

And then I had to stamp on the brakes hard, as the narrow road suddenly fell away, along with the woods. The Castle's car park lay straight ahead, and beyond that there was nothing but the cliff's edge. I brought the hire car skidding to a halt, spraying gravel in all directions, then let out my breath in a long aggrieved sigh. I looked out of the side window, and saw a small sign saying WARNING! CLIFFS AHEAD.

'Presumably the locals know when to stop and don't care about anyone else?' I said.

'A local inn for local people,' said Penny.

'Bastards, the lot of them!'

'Well, quite.'

We got out of the car and looked around. Tyrone's Castle looked exactly like the image Penny had called up on her laptop. A basic stone structure, square and blocky, under a slanting tiled roof. An effort had been made to soften the image by covering the pitted stone walls with half-timbering, but the Castle still looked more like a fortress than an inn. Built to keep the Revenue Men out rather than welcome customers in. The windows were old-fashioned leaded glass, heavy and impenetrable, but the bright light shining out seemed cheerful enough.

Three more vehicles were already parked outside the inn, set close together. None of them looked particularly stylish or interesting, just standard country runabouts. I started towards the inn, and then stopped as I stumbled over a raised concrete patch in the ground. I looked down at what turned out to be a commemorative plaque. It was pretty basic, just a raised concrete square with a blunt inscribed message: THE TYRONE HANGING TREE STOOD HERE. No date, no details. The dull-grey plaque didn't look like it had been cleaned, or even had any attention paid to it, for quite some time.

'It must have been put in place after the tree was uprooted by the storm,' said Penny. 'Not exactly decorative, is it?'

'A question occurs to me,' I said. 'Why was there only one tree outside the inn? Heavy woods lined the road all the way here, but they stopped short when the road ended. So presumably all the other trees were cleared away, apart from this one. Why would the smugglers leave only the one tree standing?'

'For the look of it?' said Penny. 'You don't always have to overthink things, Ishmael. Just because you have a naturally suspicious and paranoid mind.'

'And why put a plaque here?' I said. 'It's not flashy enough to be for the tourists, and the locals wouldn't need reminding.'

'If we were to go inside, into the nice warm pub and out of this freezing cold wind, we could probably ask someone,' said Penny, just a bit pointedly.

I looked at the cliff edge, no more than twenty feet away, and strode straight for it, ignoring the inn. I heard Penny sigh heavily and then follow reluctantly after me. The edge of the cliff was just bare stone, discoloured with age and cracked and crumbling. I came to a halt with the toes of my shoes protruding over the edge and looked out. The ocean looked back; cold and vast, its grey waters churned heavily under a grim grey sky, with just a few gulls wheeling slowly in the distance. There wasn't a ship or a sailing boat to be seen anywhere, nothing at all moving on the surface of the waters. Just the ocean, implacable and unknowable, stretching away until it finally met the sky at the horizon. A cold wind came gusting in off the sea, and I could taste salt on my lips. Penny moved in beside me and clutched firmly at my arm.

'Do you really need to stand this close to the edge, darling? Only this stone doesn't feel at all solid or reliable, and it really is an awfully long way down.'

'Heights don't bother me,' I said. 'I've never understood why heights bother anyone.'

'That's because you're an alien,' said Penny, maintaining her deathlike grip on my arm. Though whether to steady me or reassure herself wasn't clear. She glared out over the ocean, as the wind interfered with her carefully sculpted hair. 'What are you looking for, Ishmael?'

'Just trying to get a feel for the place,' I said. 'This is a really desolate spot. Not the kind of place that attracts tourists, either then or now. And look at those gulls . . . why are they so far away from land? Is there something about this location that upsets them, that drives them away?'

'Stop looking for mysteries!' said Penny. 'We're not here for that. We are on a weekend break, like any other normal couple. So act normal!'

I looked down at the narrow beach, far below. More pebbles than sand, and a hell of a lot of seaweed. Nothing to make your average tourist want to buy a bucket and spade or set up a deck chair.

'That must be where the smugglers landed their goods in the old days,' I said. 'But how did they get them off the beach and all the way up here to the inn? These are really steep cliffs.'

'I don't know,' said Penny. 'Hidden caves and tunnels, presumably? Or maybe there's a hidden stairway cut into the stone, just out of view. What does it matter? Please let's go into the Castle. This wind is blowing straight from the Arctic circle and freezing the eggs in my ovaries.'

'It's not cold,' I said. 'It's bracing. Smell that ozone.'

'You do know I could push you off this cliff edge and no one would ever convict me?'

'I think we should go inside,' I said. 'I don't know why you keep putting it off.'

We stepped back from the edge and headed for Tyrone's Castle, still comfortably arm in arm. The inn didn't get any more attractive the closer we got.

'Who else is going to be at this special meal?' I said.

Penny fished in her pocket, pulled out her letter of invitation and refreshed her memory. She's never been good with names.

'Says here . . . Jimmy Webb, reporter from the local paper. Thomas Moore, the local vicar, along with his wife Eileen. And Valerie Butler, who's writing a book about Elliot Tyrone.' She put the letter away. 'And our hosts, of course. Albert and Olivia Calvert.'

'A reporter and an author?' I said. 'You know I can't afford to appear in any kind of publicity.'

Penny squeezed my arm reassuringly against her side. 'They're here to write about the evening, not you. Forget the suspicions – we're not here on a mission, and there's no mystery to solve. We're just a normal couple out for a normal evening together.'

'We're not really a normal couple.'

'Then fake it,' said Penny. 'We're here for the meal. Nothing else.'

'A free meal,' I said. 'Always the best kind.'

'We're here to enjoy ourselves,' said Penny. 'You can do that, can't you?'

'I can do that,' I said. 'For you.'

There was only the one door to the inn, with no obvious bell or knocker, so I opened it and we walked straight in. A pleasant blast of warm air hit me in the face, along with heavy cooking smells. The bright light was particularly welcome after the increasingly grey day outside. The Castle's interior was so small there was no entrance hall. Just by walking in we'd already entered the main dining room. It was all one big open area, with a half-timbered ceiling and rough plastered walls divided into sections by thin wooden slats. There were polished floorboards, old-fashioned furniture and fittings, and horses brasses and animal-head trophies set out apparently at random. Along with a few faded black-and-white photographs and some old framed prints. Not a modern touch anywhere, apart from the efficient-looking bar tucked away at the far end of the room. Everything about the place said 'Olde worlde and proud of it'. The room felt warm and cosy, comfortable and inviting. In a rather calculated way.

The Castle might have started out as an inn, but it was now very definitely a restaurant. A dozen tables took up most of the floor, covered with gleaming white cloths. The chairs had all been carefully set in place, and there were extravagant floral displays and large unlit candles on every table. The Castle had the feel of a place where you ordered only the very best wines to complement your meal; and heaven help you if you ordered red wine with the fish.

Four people were staring coldly at Penny and me from the safety of their central table. They'd all stopped talking the moment we entered the room, and their faces were full of that 'We're local, we belong here and you don't' look common to all small town pubs. None of them said anything, even to challenge our right to be there. We were strangers – it was up to us to justify our intrusion.

'Are you sure we're invited?' I said quietly to Penny.

'We're invited,' Penny said firmly. 'Don't let them intimidate you.'

'Trust me,' I said, 'that was never on the cards.'

A side door to our left opened suddenly, and a fussy-looking man of barely medium height came bustling out. He stopped dead in his tracks when he saw us, and looked like he was about to say this was a private affair so we'd have to leave. In a really snotty voice. And then he looked more closely at Penny and his whole attitude changed. He hurried forward, smiling all over his face, positively bristling with nervous energy and professional bonhomie. He was smartly if casually dressed, well into his forties, and almost entirely bald. His face was smooth and shiny, his eyes were a faded blue, and his innkeeper's smile didn't waver once. Perhaps only I would have noticed that it didn't even come close to touching his eyes.

I really didn't like the way he was looking at Penny. As though the main course for dinner had just arrived.

'Hello! Hello!' he said, loudly and chummily. 'Albert Calvert at your service! Welcome to our special night, here at Tyrone's Castle. So glad you could make it, Penny. It has been a long time since we last saw each other, hasn't it? But I recognized you immediately!'

And then he looked pointedly at me. He was obviously surprised to see me, though he'd done his best to hide it. He'd been expecting Penny to turn up on her own.

'This is my partner, Ishmael Jones,' said Penny. 'You didn't actually say plus one on the invitation, but I didn't think you'd mind . . .'

'No! No, of course not!' Albert made a point of shaking both our hands, in a determinedly hearty manner. He turned away from me as soon as he decently could, so he could give his full attention to Penny. But not before I'd caught a rather odd look on his face. Albert had looked me over as though trying to work out whether I was going to be trouble. And if I was, whether he could handle me. I'd seen that look before, on the faces of people with good reason to be cautious of me. But I hadn't expected to encounter it in a small country pub. Albert saw me as a potential threat . . . and I had to wonder, threat to what? Penny had inherited quite a lot of money after her father's death. Did Albert hope to get his hands on some of it? Or was I just being paranoid and reading too much into one look?

No. I decided I'd keep a close eye on Albert Calvert.

He took my coat and Penny's, chatting cheerfully all the while about the length of our journey and how pleased he was we'd found the inn all right, and then hung our coats on an old-fashioned wooden coat stand by the door. It was almost buried under the coats of the four other guests, and he had to struggle to get our coats to stay put. Then he turned back and hit Penny and me with his professional smile again, rubbing his hands together briskly.

'You'll have to excuse me for a while, the wife and I are busy putting the finishing touches to the first course. You go and sit down with the others and make friends, and we'll join you soon. Lovely to have you here, Penny! We have so much to talk about. It just wouldn't have been the same without you here!'

He hurried back through the side door. Pleasant cooking smells burst out into the room and were as quickly shut off, confirming that the side door gave on to the kitchen. Penny smiled at me.

'Something smelled good.'

'Yes,' I said. 'Roast beef, dumplings and assorted vegetables, plus herbs and spices, and rather more pepper than I would have thought necessary.'

Penny looked at me. 'You got all that from one brief smell?'

'Yes.'

'Don't show me up in front of the others,' growled Penny. 'We are being normal this evening. Remember?'

'I'll do my best,' I said.

We strolled casually over to join the waiting guests, arm in arm again, to present a unified front in the face of possible enemies. The two men and two women were already on their feet, waiting to greet us. They all had welcoming smiles now Albert had vouched for us, but I could sense the strain in some of them. I nodded easily to everyone.

'Hi. I'm Ishmael Jones, and this is Penny Belcourt.'

There was a quick rush of greetings, followed by a flurry of handshakes, and then we sat down together. I couldn't help noticing that all four guests had frozen, just for a moment, when they heard Penny's name. They didn't look surprised – they'd clearly been expecting her – but something about the name had touched a nerve in each of them. And just as clearly, like Albert, they hadn't been expecting anyone to accompany her. When they looked at me, it was with open curiosity. Penny noticed their reaction, and gave them all her best dazzling smile. Which was her way of going on the offensive.

'What a delightful old inn!' she said sweetly. 'It's all so marvellously in period. Albert and Olivia are old friends of my father, Walter Belcourt. Did you know him?'

'Not personally,' said the oversized man with the vicar's white collar. 'Only through Olivia and Albert. But of course any friend of theirs . . . I'm Thomas Moore, vicar to this parish, for my sins . . .'

He chuckled richly, a warm comfortable sound. Thomas was a surprisingly muscular figure, under his black-leather motorbike jacket. He had a bluff open face, an easy-going smile, and a somewhat practised bonhomie. I had a feeling he was going to turn out to be one of those deliberately larger than life figures ('I may be a vicar, but I'm still a regular guy'). He sat in his chair as if he was at home, completely relaxed and content in all things. He had to be in his forties, and his long greying hair had been pulled back into a single thick ponytail. He nodded to the woman sitting beside him.

'This is my wife, Eileen. Couldn't manage without her. Isn't that right, dear?'

'Might help if you tried, once in a while,' Eileen said calmly, not looking at any of us. She seemed far more interested in the glass of wine in front of her.

'I didn't see a motorbike outside,' I said, nodding at Thomas's jacket.

'I love riding my bike,' he said cheerfully, 'but Eileen hates riding pillion. Don't you, dear?'

'You'll kill yourself on that thing, one of these days,' said Eileen.

She didn't sound particularly upset at the prospect. And she didn't seem all that interested in meeting Penny or me now the obligatory greetings were over. Eileen was a small, self-contained woman in her forties. Hair so blonde as to be almost colourless, no make-up on her unremarkable face, and clothes so bland as to be frankly anonymous. Either because she didn't want to stand out or because she just didn't give a damn. Everyone at the table had a glass of wine in front of them; but Eileen was the only one who hadn't let go of hers, even for a moment. She finished her wine, and put the glass down on the table with a deliberate thud.

'I want another drink.'

'We'll be eating soon, dear,' said Thomas.

'But not yet,' said Eileen. 'So get me another drink. Unless you'd rather I got it myself?'

'No, that's all right, dear, I'll get it,' said Thomas. 'Don't you stir yourself.'

He smiled quickly round the table in a 'What can you do?' sort of way, rose heavily to his feet, and went over to the bar at the far end of the room. There was a bottle of wine already standing there, and he carefully set about opening it. I'd wondered why it wasn't sitting on the table, but now I'd met Eileen I thought I knew why.

'I'm Jimmy Webb,' said the portly figure sitting opposite me. He sat slumped in his chair, almost offensively relaxed, showing off his paunch to the world and not giving a damn. Well into his forties, he wore a dark blazer and slacks and had a square self-satisfied face, topped with thinning hair gathered into a somewhat unfortunate hairstyle that fooled no one. His smile came and went without making any impression on his eyes, which didn't miss a thing. He had the air of someone just waiting for you to get something wrong, so he could rush in and correct you.

'You're the local reporter,' I said.

'Got it in one,' said Jimmy. 'No story too small, no local interest left uncovered.'

'Are you the restaurant critic for your paper?' said Penny.

Jimmy was good enough not to actually laugh in her face. 'We don't run to those kind of distinctions, my dear. We're just a small weekly rag, when all is said and done. Covering the regular grind of local events and heart-warming stories in whatever room is left after we've packed in all the advertisements. I'm the lowest on the food chain, the jack of all trades, so I handle local groups and meetings, make the most of what little crime there is, and write the horoscopes if everyone else is too busy. God help the readers of that column if I've had a bad day . . .'

'Is it interesting work?' said Penny.

'Sometimes,' said Jimmy. 'I used to dream of lucking into a big story and using it to trade up to one of the dailies, but nothing ever happens around here. The last big story in Black Rock Towen was Elliot Tyrone! I'm just a small reporter on a small paper, who never even made it on to the editorial staff. I fill a niche, I serve a purpose, and I have learned to settle for that. I volunteered to cover this special celebratory meal because Olivia and Albert are old friends. Wouldn't have missed this evening for the world.'

He toasted the closed side door with his glass, but his smile came and went even quicker than usual.

'And I'm Valerie Butler,' said the final guest at our table. 'I'm writing a book about Elliot Tyrone. About what really happened here, on that night. Because it's about time somebody did.'

Valerie was a large black woman in her forties, wearing a South American poncho of brightly-coloured patterns and intricate stitchwork over designer jeans. As though she felt obliged to appear artistic. She had a handsome face and a shaved head. And a smile aimed only at me, not Penny. There was a sense of power, of controlled strength, about Valerie. As though she was used to going after anything that mattered to her and getting it. I also had the feeling she would quite happily walk right over anyone who got in her way, and then laugh about it afterwards.

Thomas came back and placed a full glass of wine in front of Eileen. Her hand closed around it immediately, as though afraid someone might take it away. I looked around the table. All four of them were roughly the same age and they all knew each other of old. There was history between them, not all of it good. Their body language was practically shouting at me, and the occasional glances darting between them spoke volumes.

'You're obviously all old friends,' I said artlessly. 'Does that include Albert and Olivia as well?'

Various smiles came and went on their faces. Agreeing, but not as though that was necessarily a good thing. I was starting to pick up some odd emotional undercurrents among the four of them. Old secrets, old antagonisms; possibly even bad blood. I smiled inwardly. This might turn out to be an interesting evening after all.

'We're all of us local,' said Jimmy. 'We grew up together as teenagers in Black Rock Towen. Including dear Olivia and

Albert, of course. Then they went away. But now they're back, the Calverts have come home again and all is well . . .'

'The Castle used to be the best of the local pubs,' said Valerie. 'Rough as arseholes, mind you. Cheap booze that could get you hammered really quickly, bar snacks that did everything but fight back, and the pub dog was a Rottweiler.'

'It was soft as butter, once it got to know you,' said Thomas, chuckling reflectively. 'A great black beast of a dog, it would come and lean its whole weight against you and then stare at you with big loving soulful eyes. Just in case you had a crisp you weren't using. That dog would eat anything, and all evening long if you were dumb enough to let it.'

'The music was good,' said Eileen. 'And there was a special area set aside for dancing. I was so happy, then.'

'It was rough and local and frequently unpleasant,' said Jimmy. 'A fight every night, usually over a woman. And if a man didn't start it, the woman usually would. Those were the days . . . I loved the place.'

'But the townspeople weren't enough to support it,' said Valerie. 'And the tourists knew enough to stay well clear. They stuck to the more civilized places, in town. Family-friendly establishments; all charm and character, and never a raised voice. The Castle shut down some twenty years ago, and only the worst element like us missed it.'

'We weren't that bad,' said Thomas. 'Just young, and a little wild on occasion.'

'The Castle's been closed for years,' said Jimmy. 'Abandoned by the town, left alone to rot and fall apart. Everyone stayed away after that, even the local kids.'

'Of course,' said Thomas. 'They wouldn't come out here, even on a dare.'

'Really?' said Penny. 'Why not?'

The four looked at each other, suddenly uncomfortable. There was a sense of things left unsaid, because some things were best not said aloud in the presence of outsiders. In the end, Thomas shrugged heavily.

'As far as this town is concerned, the Castle has always been a bad place.'

I expected them to trot out the usual spooky stories at this point, but none of them seemed to want to say anything.

'I expected more of a presence from the local media,' I said to Jimmy. 'Just you? Not even a photographer?'

'There will be full coverage tomorrow,' said Jimmy, gratefully accepting the change of topic. 'The editor has authorized enough photos for a double-page spread to cover the grand reopening of the Castle. But tonight it's just a private gathering, for old friends. And you, of course.'

'And a chance for the Calverts to try out their culinary skills on a few amenable guinea pigs!' Thomas said cheerfully. 'To make sure everything's up to the mark before they have to serve paying customers.'

There were a few chuckles around the table; and then it all went quiet, as though the four of them had decided they'd said all they wanted to say. For a bunch of old friends, it seemed to me that none of them were exactly happy to be here. Penny took it upon herself to get the conversation started again, by smiling brightly at Valerie.

'So what was it that first interested you about the Elliot Tyrone story?'

'I wanted to know what lay behind the legend,' said Valerie, quickly warming as she embarked on her favourite subject. 'Everyone knows the story, but when I went looking for historical facts about exactly what happened here on that fateful night, I was surprised to find no one had ever written a book giving verifiable details of what the townspeople discovered when they came looking for their missing relatives. Everyone seemed to agree on the basic story, but everything else was up for grabs. So I decided if I wanted a definitive account, I'd have to write it myself.'

'Have you had many books published?' I asked politely.

'I have had a number of articles accepted,' said Valerie. 'In all kinds of magazines.'

'Some of which you might have heard of,' said Thomas.

'And some of whom might even have paid for the articles,' said Jimmy.

'This will be my first book,' Valerie said coldly. 'Several editors have expressed an interest.'

'But not quite enough to offer you an advance,' said Jimmy.

'And the Calverts don't mind that you're writing this book?' I said. 'Given that they're depending on the legend to jump-start their new business?'

'Why should they?' said Valerie.

'Because the historical facts that you discover might undermine or even discredit the legend,' I said. 'And they're going to need that to pull in the tourists.'

'People will be fascinated by what I write,' Valerie said firmly. 'Anyway, it's all publicity. And the kind of tourists attracted by the legend probably wouldn't be the kind to read my book.'

'How much of the legend is true, do you think?' asked Penny.

'Surprisingly, quite a lot of it,' said Valerie. 'Including all of the really unpleasant bits.'

'And the Voices who told Tyrone to do it?' I said.

'Who can say?' said Valerie. She stopped talking and gave her full attention to the glass of wine in front of her. As though we'd reached the limits of what she was prepared to discuss.

Jimmy leaned forward and fixed Penny with a thoughtful stare. 'Tell me, my dear, have Olivia or Albert spoken to you yet about investing your father's money in their new business?'

'No one's said anything to me about that,' said Penny.

'They will,' said Jimmy. He sank back in his chair, and drank his wine in a self-satisfied way. Happy to have spread a little mischief. 'That is why they wanted you here, when they couldn't get your father.'

'Jimmy!' said Thomas, disapprovingly.

'I'm just saying,' said Jimmy. 'A word to the wise and all that . . .'

If he was right, it was no wonder Albert had been so displeased to see Penny hadn't come on her own. It would also explain why he'd seen me as a possible threat.

Jimmy smirked to himself, satisfied that he'd thrown a cat among the pigeons. He then remembered he was supposed to be a reporter and asked Penny all the usual questions. Where are you from? What do you do? How long have you and

Ishmael been together? Penny talked a lot in return, to disguise
the fact that I wasn't saying anything. Valerie perked up when
Penny revealed that she used to be in publishing, until Penny
made it clear she no longer had any contacts in that area.

The side door slammed open again and Albert came bustling
back in to introduce his wife, Olivia. Then he quickly stepped
back to give her centre stage. One look was enough to tell me
who wore the trousers in their relationship. Some people's
body language is just deafening. And some men should wear
collars and name tags to show that they're owned. They'd
probably like it.

Olivia was a tall gangling blonde in a smart pastel-coloured
pants suit. She had a long horsey face and smiled a lot. She
moved with purpose, and had large capable hands. Like
everyone else she appeared to be in her forties, though she had
enough nervous energy for someone half her age. There was
a determined confidence to her, in her every move and look,
that was entirely missing from her husband. Olivia was used
to dealing with things. She looked at me for a long moment,
before favouring me with her version of the professional
innkeeper's smile.

'We weren't expecting you, Ishmael. Penny didn't tell us
she was bringing a friend. But of course you're very welcome.
There's more than enough food to go round!'

'I must say, I was surprised to receive your invitation,' said
Penny. 'I don't really remember you all that well, except as
old friends of my father. And that must be more than twenty
years ago.'

'That's all right, Penny,' said Olivia. 'We remember you.
And your dear father.'

Something in the way she said that caught my attention.
There was a layer of meaning in her words that I could sense,
even if I didn't understand it. Olivia and Albert both seemed
genuinely pleased that Penny had turned up for their celebratory meal, but I still wasn't entirely sure why. Something was
going on here, apart from the dinner. I made a mental note
not to leave Penny alone with the Calverts, even for a moment.

'We wish Walter could have been here tonight,' said Albert.
'So he could have seen what we've done with the old place.'

'But we're just as happy to have you here, Penny,' said Olivia.

And there it was again, a look that moved quickly among the other guests. Something they knew, something they shared, that they didn't want to discuss with Penny and me present. And given that Jimmy had already spoken so openly about lending money, what did that leave?

The Calverts didn't sit down, but seemed happy enough to hang around the table and chat amiably with their guests while the meal was cooking. The conversation moved along easily enough, and it soon became clear that the Calverts and their guests had all been very close when they were younger. Looking at faces and listening to voices, I wasn't sure that was true any more. The Calverts had left Black Rock Towen twenty years ago and this was their first time back, as the new owners of the Castle.

Thomas smiled his easy vicar's smile, and raised his glass to them. 'A toast! To Olivia and Albert, old friends returned. Welcome back!'

Everyone echoed the toast, and drank willingly enough. But Jimmy smiled sardonically, Valerie smiled politely, and Eileen didn't smile at all. And the Calverts . . . didn't appear to feel particularly flattered. As though the toast was a dig at them for having gone away. Olivia gave Albert a hard look, urging him to say something.

'We've done our best to recreate the interior of the Castle exactly as it was in Elliot Tyrone's time,' Albert said quickly. 'Apart from the kitchen and the bar, of course. Health and Safety put their foot down there.'

'But otherwise, everything you see here is exactly as it used to be,' said Olivia, 'based on the best evidence our researches could turn up. It wasn't easy. There's been quite a lot written about the murders, but very little about what the Castle actually looked like back then.'

'Just a few old drawings,' said Albert, 'in a local history that predated the murders. But everything in here is accurate for the year 1886.'

'Do you know what Tyrone himself looked like?' said Penny.

'Oh yes,' said Albert. And then he stopped and looked

quickly at his wife, to check if she wanted to be the one to tell it. She nodded brusquely to him, and he hurried on. 'There weren't any photographs, but we did find a black-and-white illustration from a popular magazine of the time.'

He pointed proudly to a framed drawing on the wall by the bar. It showed Elliot Tyrone as a large, hulking, powerful figure in standard innkeeper's outfit, his apron spattered with blood. He had a harsh, scowling face, and dark piercing eyes. He looked like someone who'd poison a room full of people and then blame it on the Voices.

'I don't suppose he looked that bad in real life,' said Olivia, 'or no one would have gone to his inn! Most accounts agree that up until that night Tyrone was a well-liked and respected figure in the community.'

'The drawing was commissioned after his death,' said Valerie. 'Based on descriptions by people who knew him. The incident was bound to have affected their perception of him.'

'Something must have got to Tyrone,' said Eileen.

'Or someone,' said Thomas.

'But no one knows who,' said Jimmy. 'It's a mystery.'

'The real mystery is what happened to Tyrone's wife and two teenage daughters,' said Valerie. 'There was no sign of them anywhere in the Castle when the townspeople arrived . . . So did Tyrone kill them first and hide their bodies? They've never been found, even after all these years. Or did they discover what he was planning to do and run for their lives? But if that was the case, where did they go? I couldn't find any trace of them in the surrounding towns, and I searched through all the local parish records for their names.'

'They probably took to their heels the moment they realized he was going crazy,' said Jimmy. 'Got as far away from here as they could and then changed their names so they could make a new life for themselves. So none of what Tyrone did could attach itself to them.'

'You really think Tyrone would have let them run?' said Olivia.

'What do you think happened?' I said.

Albert shrugged, Olivia smiled. 'Just another of the many

mysteries and talking points that will bring in the tourists,' she said cheerfully.

I looked to Valerie. 'What do you think happened?'

To my surprise she hesitated. And Jimmy was quick to get in first, smiling his self-satisfied smile.

'I made it my business to look up the old details in my newspaper's morgue. All the original stories in our dusty archives. Just to refresh my memory and make sure I could hold my own during the evening's conversation. The first killings in the Castle took place a century or more before Tyrone. When Revenue Men stormed the inn to bring down the local smugglers, who'd made the mistake of becoming too successful to be overlooked any longer. Bit of a bloodbath by all accounts. The smugglers barricaded themselves inside this stony edifice, but the Revenue Men had the numbers and forced their way in. The smugglers fought it out, and lost. The few survivors were summarily hanged from the tree outside. The Castle was sold off at public auction and new owners took it on, as just an inn.'

'I wouldn't have thought they'd have many customers, after so many people died here,' said Penny.

'Not at all!' said Olivia. 'People came from far and wide, just to see where the battle took place. The general public has always liked a good bloody story. That's what we're counting on.'

'But custom gradually faded away,' said Albert, 'As newer and bloodier stories caught the public's attention. The Castle became yesterday's news and settled for being just another country pub. Until Elliot Tyrone made the place infamous again.'

'And now Tyrone's story is old enough to be new again,' said Olivia. 'We're spreading the story through our website, plus local publicity. A horror story this good is bound to bring the tourists back.'

'They'll come for the story, but they'll stay for our cooking,' said Albert.

I smiled. 'I wonder if that's what Tyrone said . . .'

Penny glared at me.

'I have turned up some new information during my extensive researches,' said Valerie, determined not to be left out of things.

'Jimmy was kind enough to allow me access to his newspaper stacks, and I found all kinds of interesting things that never made it into the regular story.'

'Of course he let you have access,' said Eileen, as much to her glass as anyone else. 'He never could refuse you anything.'

'I always thought I had a book in me,' said Jimmy, just a bit loudly. 'But I never could find the time.'

'I've been trying to work out who or what the Voices might have been that Tyrone swore drove him to kill all those people,' said Valerie, talking right over Jimmy. 'I found a memoir written by one of the men who helped hang Elliot Tyrone. He said he asked Tyrone about the Voices, and Tyrone said they just came to him out of nowhere. So sudden and so powerful he was helpless before them. Now, if he'd been suffering from some kind of mental illness you'd expect him to have been hearing the Voices for some time. This account makes it sound more like he was possessed . . .'

I looked around the table. Everyone was listening carefully, their faces blank. 'Do you have any idea who or what the Voices might have been?' I said. 'Are there any local superstitions to account for them?'

'It was the Devil,' said Thomas. His voice was quite calm and matter of fact.

'There are some local stories,' said Valerie, ostentatiously ignoring Thomas. 'But there's not much to them. There are two celebrated local witches from the same time as the smugglers, though their fame never travelled much beyond the town. The first one, Nettie of the Woods, might or might not have been a gypsy. People who hear her voice in the woods are supposed to go mad with fear and run till they drop. The other one was called Agnes of the Well, though who she was or where the well was are lost to us now. Agnes was supposed to whistle up storms to drown the local fishermen. Just for the joy and the spite of it, apparently. And there's been reports of selkies off the coast for generations. They are the Cornish version of mermaids, though they're supposed to be shape-shifters too.'

'All very interesting, I'm sure,' said Jimmy, in a tone that suggested otherwise. 'But what reason could any of them have to make an innkeeper poison his guests?'

'They're just stories,' said Valerie. 'And who knows what details might have been lost down the years?'

'I did some research myself, once I knew I was coming down here,' said Penny. 'Several local murderers have blamed the Voices, haven't they? Did any of them ever put a name to the Voice they heard?'

'No,' said Jimmy. 'Not one of them. You're very well informed, my dear.'

'I was interested,' said Penny.

'What about ghost stories?' I said. 'Every old inn worth its salt comes with a few ghost stories attached. I know about the tree, but what about inside the inn? Has Tyrone ever been seen walking about, or any of his victims? Or any of the smugglers who died here?'

'Surprisingly, no,' said Valerie. 'But there have been any number of sightings of the hanging tree, back in its old place. Right up to modern times. Odd, really, given how many people have died in this inn. I'm surprised we're not hip deep in ghosts.'

Everyone round the table laughed.

'You don't believe in ghosts?' I said.

They all gave me the same pitying look.

'It's all just stuff made up for the tourists,' said Olivia. 'No one around here believes any of that nonsense. We just tell the old tales to keep the tourists happy. So they can take the stories home with them, along with their overpriced souvenirs.'

'Tyrone's story will make the Castle very popular,' said Albert.

'You've put a lot of effort into refurbishing this place,' said Jimmy. 'Must have cost a bit to get all the details right. Where did you find that kind of money?'

The question was clearly meant to sound casual. But it came out a little too sharply, as though Jimmy had a point to make. Albert just smiled happily back at him.

'We won the lottery!'

'Not the big prize, obviously,' said Olivia. 'We're not million-aires, or we wouldn't need to run a pub, would we? But we won enough to make it possible for us to buy the Castle and renovate it from top to bottom. We always wanted to do that.'

And again, a look moved quickly among the four guests. They knew something I didn't, and I was getting pretty tired of that.

'Of course,' said Jimmy, entirely casually, 'if your grand opening tomorrow turns out to be a flop – perhaps because I write a really bad review of tonight's meal – that would ruin your big comeback, wouldn't it?'

Among old friends that should have been a joke, just a bit of banter. But instead, it sounded almost like a threat. Olivia smiled easily back at him.

'We expect most of our business to come from outside the area. Our website should bring people here from all over the country. That's where the real money is. So you can write whatever you like, Jimmy, it won't make any difference. You just relax and enjoy yourself.'

'People love old horror stories these days,' Albert said comfortably. 'And we've got one of the best.'

'I'm not sure I approve of using the legend of Elliot Tyrone like this,' said Thomas. 'It was a terrible chapter in the town's history.'

'Good thing we don't need your approval then, Thomas,' said Olivia.

'Your opening night is practically a celebration of murder,' Thomas said flatly.

'It all happened a long time ago,' said Albert.

'There are still people living in Black Rock Towen today who had relatives die here on that awful night,' said Eileen. 'They still remember.'

'Then they should stay away,' Olivia said lightly, 'so they won't be upset. We can manage without their custom.'

'I have to wonder,' said Thomas, 'whether it could be dangerous reviving Tyrone's past? Rebuilding the scene of his crime, calling on his name . . . Sometimes the past should be left in the past, so it won't return to trouble the present. How can anything good come of something so evil?'

'There's nothing to worry about,' Olivia said firmly. 'All the time Albert and I have spent here overseeing the renovations, neither of us have ever seen or heard anything out of the ordinary.'

'Though you had to bring in builders from outside,' said Eileen. 'From the city. Because no one local would do the work, for any amount of money.'

'Why is that?' asked Penny.

'Because this is a bad place,' said Eileen. 'Always has been. And everyone in the town knows it.'

'We went to the city for our workforce because we wanted experienced professionals,' said Olivia. 'Not just local joiners and plasterers. Everything here had to be historically accurate, right down to the smallest detail.'

'Even though it did use up most of our money,' said Albert. 'Of course, we did experience a few unusual things . . .'

'What sort of things?' Penny asked immediately.

'Nothing, really,' said Olivia, frowning at Albert. 'Just . . . sometimes things would go missing. I would put something down, and when I turned back it was gone. They always turned up later.'

'Perhaps we've got a very tidy poltergeist . . .' said Albert.

Everyone laughed, except Thomas. The vicar was looking unusually solemn. Almost disturbed.

'There was an exorcism here, you know,' he said. 'They brought in a bishop, from Truro, and he did the whole bell, book and candle thing. That was just a few weeks after the murders. Because of what Tyrone said, about the Voices.'

'Did the exorcism have any effect?' I said.

'No,' said Thomas. 'It didn't. I'm pretty sure it was all put on for show. To reassure people that it was safe to patronize the Castle again. The new owner probably called in a favour.'

'But it was still a bad place,' said Eileen. 'They had to call in a second bishop just a year later.'

'Yes,' said Thomas. 'All the way from London. Whatever could have been happening here to bring a bishop all the way down to Cornwall in those times?'

'I didn't know there was a second exorcism,' said Jimmy. He looked at Valerie. 'Did you know?'

'No,' she said. 'There wasn't anything about that in the local press . . .'

Thomas smiled. 'It's in the Church records. Everything's there if you know where to look.'

'Why did you look?' I said.

'Because nothing good can come of a celebration of murder,' said Thomas.

'Then why are you here?' said Olivia.

'Because I thought you might need me,' Thomas said evenly. 'Eileen's quite right, this is a bad place. Not just the inn. Did you know that this whole area is infamous for having the highest number of missing persons in the country? Every year people disappear and are never seen again.'

'That's easy enough to explain,' said Jimmy. 'They've all gone off to the cities, where the jobs are!'

He laughed, but nobody joined in. They were all looking thoughtful. Olivia's head came up sharply.

'Oh! Look at the time! You'll have to excuse us, the first course is almost ready.'

She disappeared back through the side door, followed quickly by Albert.

'After all this build-up, the meal had better be pretty damned memorable,' said Jimmy.

'I'm sure it will be,' said Thomas.

# THREE

## The Past is Always With Us

The side door slammed open again and Albert came bustling back in, pushing a heavily-laden trolley ahead of him. Wafts of steam and pleasant odours rose up from plates of food and a wide assortment of side dishes. Olivia followed Albert in and oversaw his distribution of the meal. She didn't actually do anything to help, but no doubt her constant running commentary helped Albert do his job. Plates piled high with good food appeared before all of us in quick succession, followed by two Victorian-period gravy boats and all kinds of extra vegetables. Sounds of hearty appreciation rose on every side at the sight and smells of the grand celebratory meal. Which turned out to be exactly what I had identified earlier from the kitchen aromas – thickly sliced roast beef and plenty of it, big fluffy dumplings, and a satisfyingly wide assortment of out-of-season vegetables. All of it nicely perked up with herbs and spices and more pepper than I would have considered strictly necessary, though no one else seemed to notice that last bit or give a damn.

'Traditional olde English fare,' Olivia said proudly. 'Taken from an actual menu prepared by Elliot Tyrone himself.'

'Then maybe we should get in a food taster,' Jimmy said loudly. 'Just to be on the safe side . . .'

Various smiles and chuckles greeted his attempt at humour. Olivia made a point of forking a small portion of Jimmy's food from off his plate and chewing it thoroughly. Jimmy had the grace to look a little abashed, even though he couldn't bring himself to apologize. Thomas gave him a stern look, and then everyone gave their full attention to the meal. We all tried the meal carefully at first, ready to make polite comments if any of the food turned out to be a disappointment. But it was all excellent stuff and we all tucked in happily. Albert and Olivia sat down together at the far end of the table and seemed to spend as much time watching everyone for their reactions as they did eating. We were all careful to smile widely and make appreciative noises, and disputed vigorously over extra helpings from the side dishes. Sometimes, it's a hard job being a guest.

Bottles of wine had appeared along with the food, a nice assortment of acceptable reds. Good enough for no one to feel like allowing the wine time to breathe. Eileen immediately grabbed hold of a bottle and planted it firmly in front of her, so she could refill her glass whenever she felt like it. Thomas watched her do this, but didn't say anything. As though it was just normal behaviour where Eileen was concerned. He didn't appear upset or disappointed, just quietly resigned. I had to wonder how long this had been going on. I did notice that even though Eileen had been putting back the booze at a steady rate for some time, she didn't seem particularly affected. And it certainly didn't interfere with her appetite for the food in front of her.

Conversation rose and fell around the table, slowed down by our enjoyment of the food but not stopped. The newly reunited old friends had a lot to say, though I got the impression that sometimes what wasn't being said was just as significant as what was. I was fascinated by the way they all circled around and even avoided subjects I would have expected them to care about most. They talked about the food, of course, along with remembered good times and old exploits . . . But no one talked about what the four guests were doing for a living these days, or what they were planning to do. What kind of old friends aren't interested in catching up? And, most intriguing of all, not a word was spoken about the legend of Elliot Tyrone or the inn's past history.

I was still waiting for Albert and Olivia to explain why they'd invited Penny to attend. Everyone went out of their way to include her and me in the general conversation, but I couldn't help listening for the other shoe to drop. In the end, I just concentrated on my food and didn't press the point. I was glad of a chance for the two of us to relax, away from the weird business and unnatural mysteries that took up most of our time together and enjoying being a normal couple on a normal night out.

Valerie was sitting on my other side. Suddenly she leaned over and forked a little something from my plate. When I looked at her, she just smiled and popped the morsel into her mouth with a decidedly sensual flourish. I smiled back at her uncertainly. Then without waiting for me to ask or even indicate whether I wanted more wine, she filled my glass to the brim. I nodded my thanks in a carefully non-committal way, not sure where this was going. Valerie then leaned in really close, so she could remark on how good the food was, how well the evening was going, and how pleased she was that I was there. She placed her hand on top of mine and stared directly into my eyes. I did my best to make polite replies and not let her see how baffled I was by her behaviour. She was after something. But what? I waited till she turned away to pour herself more wine, then withdrew my hand from under hers and turned to Penny, who had clearly seen it all and was grinning broadly at my discomfort. I raised an eyebrow, to ask what was going on.

Penny leaned in close, and I put my head forward so she could murmur in my ear.

'She fancies you, you idiot . . .'

I shook my head slowly. Even after all these years, there were certain subtleties of human behaviour that still escaped me. Penny might find it all very amusing, but I didn't. I shifted my chair away from Valerie and closer to Penny. Valerie turned back in time to see this and shrugged briefly, then switched her attention to Jimmy, sitting opposite her. She thanked him for all his help in researching her book and giving her a lift to the Castle in his car, and made a point of telling him how much she'd enjoyed a particular article he'd written recently. And all the time her hand was on top of his, while she stared straight into his eyes. Jimmy didn't seem to find anything unusual in this behaviour. He smiled easily back at her and promised he would do whatever he could to help her. Thomas hadn't missed any of this, and was smiling privately. Eileen had also noticed, but didn't appear to give a damn.

The conversation hit a natural lull and silence fell across

the table. Perhaps only I seemed to notice how uncomfortable this made everyone else. As if gaps couldn't be allowed, in case someone filled them with the wrong subject. Thomas cleared his throat, and turned to face Albert and Olivia.

'So where have the two of you been keeping yourselves all these years you've been away?'

Albert and Olivia looked at each other quickly. I had the impression that Albert was silently asking Olivia whether she wanted to speak first. And when she made it clear she didn't, just how much he should say. She intimated that he should get on with it, but be careful what he said. It's amazing how much you can pack into a couple of quick looks.

'We've been living in London,' said Albert. 'Involved in a series of small businesses. Some successful, others not so much. Everything from running a small publishing firm and running murder mysteries to running a small bed and breakfast . . . Never really doing what we wanted, but following opportunities and making a living.'

'Whereabouts in London?' asked Jimmy, tearing his gaze away from Valerie as his reporter's instincts kicked in.

'Never any of the fashionable areas,' said Albert. 'A good address can look very impressive on a business card, but it'll cost you an arm and a leg. We were doing all right, but we were never really satisfied . . . until our lottery win gave us the opportunity to return home.'

'And achieve our old dream, at last,' said Olivia.

'We had such hopes and plans when we were younger!' said Thomas. 'There were so many things we were going to do . . . We were going to make something of ourselves and change the world! What happened to us?'

'We grew up,' said Eileen.

Another silence fell, that no one seemed to want to break. But since Penny has never allowed good manners to get in the way when she wants to know something, she proceeded to press Thomas on what he'd been saying.

'Didn't you always want to be a vicar?'

He laughed, apparently quite genuinely. 'No! I wanted to race motorbikes for a living. Or failing that, I wanted to work on them as a mechanic. But I experienced my own "Road to

Damascus" conversion, my very own moment of spiritual insight and understanding. It opened my eyes and changed the way I saw the world forever . . . I was suddenly aware that there was so much more to life.'

'What happened?' said Penny.

'He ate some mushrooms,' said Eileen.

'The cause isn't important,' Thomas said firmly. 'What matters is that my inner eyes had been forced all the way open. And once I had been forced to acknowledge the possibility of a much larger world, I couldn't look away. I had a head full of questions, and no answers. And wanted to know more. So I dropped everything, considered the possibilities, and entered a seminary. To study and to assure myself that I had a real vocation. Somewhat to my surprise, I discovered that I did. Afterwards I could have applied for a parish anywhere, but I chose to return to Black Rock Towen. Because that was where my roots were, and because I thought I could make a difference here. It's hard to make an impression on people in a big city – there are too many distractions and your efforts get spread too thin. But in a small town like this, one man can make a difference. Besides, Eileen was here.'

'And so I became a vicar's wife,' said Eileen. She smiled briefly. There was something in her eyes that might have been sadness. Maybe bitterness. 'Even though that was never on the list of things that I hoped to be someday.'

'Was there something else you would rather have been?' asked Penny.

'I never could decide,' said Eileen. She drank unhurriedly from her glass, as she gave the question some serious thought. 'I was always ready to go along with whatever anyone else wanted and what other people thought I should be. And while I was still trying to make up my mind, life happened and I found I was stuck . . .'

Before another silence could fall, or perhaps because he was worried where Eileen's thoughts might be leading her, Jimmy decided to butt in.

'I always knew I wanted to be a journalist. To find out what was really going on in the world and tell people all about it. To wake them up and make them take notice. When I got my

job on the local rag, I thought that was just a stepping stone
to bigger stories on bigger papers . . . But somehow the opportunity to move on and move up never happened. So here I
am, telling people things they probably already know. And
don't care that much about anyway, as long as I spell their
names right.'

'You could have left the town any time,' said Valerie.

'I always meant to,' said Jimmy. 'But life got in the way.
You never left, either . . .'

'Black Rock Towen has a hold on all of us,' said Valerie.
'And the big world can seem a very scary place when all
you've ever known is a small town.'

I looked at Albert and Olivia. 'You left . . .'

'We had to,' said Albert. 'We had no choice.'

There was a quiet but very real bitterness in his tone. Olivia
shot him a hard look, before smoothly taking over.

'We had no choice if we were to make something of
ourselves. But now here we are, back again, to make our dream
come true at last!'

'Not all of us can afford dreams,' said Jimmy. 'Some of us
have to settle for what we can get.'

I sensed a certain frisson around the table, among the four
guests. A quiet sadness, of dreams given up on.

Jimmy glowered suddenly at Penny. 'We can't all inherit a
fortune from father.'

He realized the others were all staring at him and that he'd
gone too far, but he just scowled defiantly back. Albert cleared
his throat and nudged Olivia's arm. She gave him an 'I know,
I hadn't forgotten' look.

She produced a small bottle of plum brandy and presented
it to me with a flourish. 'A speciality of the inn, Ishmael. A
little something from Tyrone's time. Do try some. I'd appreciate
your opinion.'

She uncorked the bottle and poured a generous measure
into a fresh glass. The brandy was a delicate tawny shade and
smelled distinctly fruity. I didn't see any point in telling Olivia
that I'd never developed any opinions about good or bad booze,
because none of it has ever had any effect on me. So I just
savoured the aroma appreciatively and swilled the stuff around

in my mouth as if I knew what I was doing. In my line of work, you learn to fake all kinds of things.

'Excellent,' I said solemnly. 'A good nose, a fine body, and a surprisingly evocative aftertaste.'

I can talk the talk when I have to. I drank the stuff down, and Olivia immediately poured me some more, filling my glass right to the brim. I wondered if she was trying to get me drunk so she and Albert could gang up on Penny. In which case, they were on a hiding to nothing. I could drink brandy by the gallon and not even slur my speech. I emptied my glass, and Olivia poured me some more. And we both smiled happily at each other, each of us thinking our own thoughts.

'I am pleased you and Albert have taken over the Castle, Olivia,' said Thomas. 'A prosperous and successful Castle can only be good for all of us.'

Jimmy looked at him dubiously. 'How do you make that out?'

'You'll get a whole series of stories for your paper,' said Thomas. 'About the return of the prodigals, and the inn's colourful history, and all the tourists it will attract to Black Rock Towen. A successful relaunching of Tyrone's legend will undoubtedly help sales of Valerie's book. And I will be glad to see more tourist money coming in, which will help the local economy and improve the townspeople's lives.'

'You're always so selfless, Thomas,' said Eileen.

'Part of the job, dear.'

'And what about me?' said Eileen. 'What do I get out of all this?'

'Somewhere new to drink,' said Thomas.

For the first time, there was a certain sharpness in his voice. Eileen looked at him and raised her glass in salute to acknowledge the point.

We'd all finished eating by now, including extra helpings from the lower shelves of the trolley, and we sat back in our chairs, happy and full and satisfied. We smiled at each other, and nodded appreciatively to our hosts.

'That was a fine meal,' said Thomas. 'And a good end to the long shadow cast by Tyrone's last celebration.' But then he frowned, looking thoughtfully at Albert and Olivia. 'Still,

I have to ask – do you really think it's a good idea to publicize the more unpleasant aspects of that man's story, just to drag people in? Your culinary skills are good enough to make the inn a success, all on their own.'

'These days it's important to have a gimmick,' said Olivia. 'If you're to stand out from all the other country inns and themed restaurants.'

'But which part of the legend are you going to concentrate on?' said Thomas, pushing the point. 'The murders? Or the supernatural element?'

'It's all just stories . . .' said Albert.

'I was wondering about that,' said Penny. 'I've heard so many stories tonight about Tyrone and the inn. They can't all be true. I'm still not clear about this whole Voices thing . . .'

'It's just local traditions,' said Valerie. 'There are whole cycles of old legends covering the same ground over and over again. People have been hearing Voices in this vicinity for generations. In the woods, out at sea . . . Sometimes right in the middle of the town in the quiet hours of the night.'

'But what do these Voices have to say?' I asked.

'Depends on which version of the stories you listen to,' said Jimmy. 'Sometimes it's threats, sometimes it's temptations; other times it's personal stuff. Warnings about enemies, confirmation of gossip, things you should and shouldn't do . . . Stories tailored to suit the needs and morals of their times. They're just small-town scares designed to keep people in line.'

'A lot of the time, yes, I would have to agree with that,' said Thomas. 'Stories crafted to serve a moral purpose and reinforce local customs.'

'You're actually agreeing with me?' said Jimmy. 'Quick, somebody take a photo . . .'

'Who'd know better about such things than me?' said Thomas. 'The whole Church is based on parables, after all. But there is one local story that strikes true to me. Very different to all the others, though not unconnected . . .'

'There is?' said Jimmy. 'Do tell, Thomas. This is all news to me.'

Valerie leaned forward across the table, fixing Thomas with

her gaze. 'And to me. I thought I'd covered all the local legends in my research. What did I miss?'

Thomas stirred uncomfortably as we all looked at him curiously. As if he was suddenly unsure whether he should have raised the subject. He looked at his wine glass, but didn't touch it. And then he smiled calmly round the table and relaxed in his chair, as he decided to go ahead. His heavy black-leather jacket made soft creaking noises as he settled himself comfortably.

'This is another story I discovered in the old Church records. I spent a lot of time going through them after I returned to Black Rock Towen. Trying to immerse myself in the spirit of the place after so long away. Anyway . . . this particular tale dates back to the middle of the seventeenth century. It seems a certain scholar of great renown came to Black Rock Towen, searching for a certain rare book he thought he might find in our justly famous old town library. Impressed by his reputation, the worthy overseers of the town library allowed him unfettered access. According to the reports I read, he eventually discovered the book he was looking for, and used what he found in it for purposes the town elders would never have approved of. He is supposed to have made a pact with some unknown force and opened a door between this world and another. And something came through, or got out.

'Some say it's still here after all these years . . . something unseen and perhaps even bodiless, trapped in our world. And the Voices people hear are this unnatural creature taking out its anger on us, because the door closed and it can't get back to where it belongs. Now it's just a Voice in the night, speaking evil. Because that's all that's left of it.'

There was a long pause. Everyone looked at everyone else and waited for someone to say something.

'What happened to the renowned scholar?' asked Penny.

'There's nothing in the records about that,' said Thomas. 'Even his name has been expunged. Perhaps he found out the hard way that a door opens both ways.'

Jimmy applauded loudly, in an only somewhat condescending manner. 'Well done, Thomas! I never knew you were such a great storyteller!'

'He isn't usually,' said Eileen. 'Have you ever listened to one of his sermons? No, of course not. Silly question.'

'I don't bother Thomas where he works, and he doesn't bother me at the paper,' said Jimmy. 'If only the rest of the world would follow our example.'

'I can see I'm going to have to investigate these old Church records of yours, Thomas,' said Valerie, cutting in quickly. 'You will allow me access, won't you?'

'Ask me later,' said Thomas.

'I'm still not clear about why people made such a point of staying away from the Castle while it was empty and run down,' I said. 'If no one's ever seen a ghost around here, apart from the tree, of course . . . What keeps the local youths away? I would have thought a reputation as a bad place would have acted like catnip to kids looking for some mischief to get into. So what scares them off?'

There was another long pause, but this time the silence around the table felt distinctly uncomfortable.

'Some stories are all the more unpleasant because they're true,' Thomas said finally. 'Matters of undeniable fact, not legend. This particular story happened not long after Albert and Olivia left Black Rock Towen. The Castle was empty, deserted, but not yet the ruin it was destined to become.'

He paused, and Olivia forced a smile. 'You can't stop there, Thomas! What is it? What happened? If this involves the Castle, if it's something that could affect our business, then Albert and I need to know. Why do the local kids stay away?'

'A couple of boys came out here late one evening,' Thomas said heavily. 'Eleven years old, and already well-known trouble-makers. Looking to make a name for themselves with their peers by indulging in a little criminal damage. Broken windows, graffiti, the usual. Maybe even break into the Castle and see if there was anything worth stealing. Two boys came out here, but only one came back. By then it was the early hours of the morning. Their parents had finally noticed their absence and raised the alarm. People were standing around in the main street, arguing over where to start their search, when one of the boys came staggering back into town. White-faced, trembling all over, with eyes like he'd looked into Hell itself

'. . . It took some time before he was able to answer questions. He said his friend had stepped off the edge of the cliff. Not fallen, or even jumped. Just deliberately stepped out into nothing and fell to his death.'

'Why would he do something like that?' said Penny.

'You know why . . .' said Eileen. 'The Voices told him to.'

Thomas nodded slowly. 'That was the boy's story. And he stuck to it, no matter how hard people pressed him.'

'What happened to the boy?' I asked.

'He hanged himself,' said Thomas. 'And that's why even today no one from town likes to come out here once it gets dark. Even though none of them will admit it.' He smiled bleakly at Albert and Olivia. 'Not a story to put on your website. The tourists wouldn't like it.'

'This is a bad place,' said Eileen. 'Always has been. Nothing good will ever come of it.'

Olivia scowled at her, not bothering to hide the anger in her voice. 'There's nothing in any way weird or supernatural happening here! Nothing! The stories . . . are just stories! The kid who fell was probably pushed over the edge by his friend, and that's why he hanged himself. Look, Albert and I both slept here overnight in the guest rooms upstairs when we were overseeing the renovation, and neither of us ever saw or heard anything. Tell them, Albert!'

And then she glared at him, when he didn't immediately back her up. Albert shifted in his chair, clearing his throat reluctantly as everyone stared at him.

'I never actually saw anything,' he said. 'But I did hear things occasionally . . .'

'Like what?' Penny asked immediately.

Albert looked at his wife, to see if he should continue. She shrugged testily and gave him a 'Go ahead if you want to make a fool of yourself' look. Albert took a long drink from his glass before facing the rest of us.

'More than once, in the night, I was sure I heard footsteps. Walking back and forth, down here. At first I put it down to creakings in the wooden floor, or to the structure of the inn settling after all the changes we'd made. But it did sound very much like footsteps.'

For the first time, I felt like taking him seriously. Substantial changes to the physical structure of an old building have been known to bring about all kinds of intrusions from the past. Like playing back an old recording. Which is as close as I was ever going to come to accepting a ghost.

'Did you ever go downstairs to check?' Penny asked Albert.

'Just the once,' he said slowly. 'Olivia never heard anything. She's a very deep sleeper. The footsteps sounded particularly loud and distinct that night, and I was concerned it might be an intruder. So I put on my dressing gown and came downstairs. Making lots of noise on the stairs, so if anyone was down here they'd have plenty of time to get out. But when I entered the dining room and turned on the lights, the place was empty. Nothing to show anyone had ever been in here . . .'

I looked at Olivia and she shrugged, unimpressed. 'I never heard anything in the night.'

'But you did see something,' Albert said stubbornly.

Olivia glared at him as though he'd let her down, before looking reluctantly round the table. 'It wasn't anything, really. It was just that now and again I would find one of the guest-room doors standing open when I was sure I'd closed it. But I could have been mistaken, or the door could simply have been hung badly. Nothing to get excited about. I have never seen or heard anything supernatural in this inn! Not once!'

'But there are all these stories . . .' said Penny.

'And that's all they are! Just stories!' Olivia stopped, and took a moment to compose herself before continuing. 'It's all just made-up stuff, tall tales to please the tourists. I don't mind using the old legends to pull in the customers, but I draw the line at taking any of this nonsense seriously. Or letting it get to me. Such things just don't happen in the real world.' She looked at me challengingly. 'Do you believe in the supernatural?'

'The supernatural?' I said. 'No.'

'It's true,' said Penny. 'He really doesn't. But don't get him started on the paranormal.'

'I saw a ghost, once,' said Eileen.

We all stopped, and turned to stare at her. Eileen's voice had been almost offhand. Calm and matter of fact.

'A ghost?' said Thomas. He looked startled, even shocked. 'Here, in the Castle?'

'Of course not here,' said Eileen. She took a reflective drink from her glass, and then put it down and looked composedly round the table. 'I was just a child, eight years old. I woke up in my bed in the early hours of the morning. It was summer, so it was already light. I could see my room quite clearly. I just lay there for a while, waiting to go back to sleep, when I saw something standing at the foot of my bed, looking at me. It was just a dark shape, a human figure, but far too tall. There was something wrong in the way it stood . . . But I was so young. You just accept things, at that age. I closed my eyes and looked again, and it was gone. I didn't make a fuss. Just went back to sleep.

'At breakfast, I tried to tell my mother what I'd seen. She said it must have been my father, looking in to check I was all right. But I knew what my father looked like. What I'd seen didn't look anything like him. Then she said I must have been dreaming. So I just nodded, and got on with my cereal. I knew better than to argue, even at that age. But it didn't feel like a dream. A dream can fool you into thinking it's real, but only while you're dreaming. Once you're awake, you know what's real and what isn't. I know what I saw.'

She stopped for a moment, her eyes far away, intent on yesterday. 'I can still see that dark shape in my mind's eye, as clearly as I saw it then, all those years ago. And I don't know what else to call it apart from a ghost.'

She smiled briefly round the table, and then returned her attention to her glass of wine.

'Did you ever see this figure again?' said Penny.

'No,' said Eileen.

'You never told me any of this before,' said Thomas.

'You never asked,' said Eileen.

'What is the Church's official position on ghosts, in these modern times?' I asked Thomas.

He surprised me by considering the question seriously. 'We take a case by case position. Officially, the Church likes to appear open-minded. More things in Heaven and Earth and all that. But unofficially, at the very top of the pecking order, where all the important decisions are made, it has been made very clear that they don't want to know . . . They don't want to have to get involved with anything that might rock the boat. With things they can't explain, that don't fit into their comfortable world view. Ghosts and ghoulies smack too much of the old superstitions that we're all supposed to have put behind us. We're a modern Church now. The Devil is dead. Evil is psychological.'

'But what do you believe?' I said bluntly. I was genuinely interested in what his answer would be.

Thomas smiled suddenly. 'You know, I think I'd quite like to meet a ghost. So I could talk to it and ask it questions.'

'You'd run a mile,' said Eileen.

Thomas let out a brief bark of laughter. 'Probably!'

The mood around the table lightened perceptibly. Jimmy fixed me with a challenging smirk.

'What about you, Ishmael? Do you believe in ghosts?'

'No,' I said firmly.

'It's true,' said Penny. 'Even though he believes in all sorts of other things.'

'Such as?' said Jimmy.

'I could tell you,' I said. 'But then I'd have to haunt you.'

Everyone contemplated their drinks for a while, sitting quietly. I finished my brandy, and Olivia emptied the last of the bottle into my glass. I was surprised to find I'd drunk it all. Olivia was looking at me expectantly, as if trying to determine how much the plum brandy was affecting me. I smiled easily back at her. I was feeling pretty good; full of good food, enjoying the pleasant setting, and happily engaged in trying to sort out all the past and present emotional entanglements of the six old friends sitting around me.

It should have been a happy reunion, after all these years. But I wasn't convinced. There was something they weren't telling me. Or each other.

The room felt warm and cosy, the inn's thick stone walls protecting us from the cold night and the rising wind outside. No one seemed to feel like talking. We were all comfortable with the quiet, sitting back in our chairs happily digesting our meal. I looked around the room, at the meticulously recreated setting of Tyrone's day, and it didn't look in the least dangerous or threatening. Or in any way supernaturally challenged. Just an old country pub where you could always be sure of finding a cheerful welcome, excellent food and pleasant company. Penny was right: it did make a nice change, to be able to relax like everyone else.

The stories were obviously just stories. Like all the others I'd been told down the years, so similar they were practically generic. Everywhere you go you can hear stories just like them, with variations according to the setting and local preoccupations. And the few things Albert and Olivia had encountered in the inn were just too ordinary for words. I was actually considering asking the Calverts if Penny and I might spend the night at the Castle, in one of the guest rooms upstairs. Better than a long drive back to our hotel.

And then Jimmy leaned forward in his chair and fixed Albert and Olivia with a beady gaze. His face was a little flushed, and even before he opened his mouth I knew he was going to say something he shouldn't. Because he just couldn't help himself. Something had been building up all evening, something from out of the past, and he just couldn't hold it in any longer.

'So, Olivia,' he said loudly, 'are you ready to tell Penny why you really wanted her here?'

His voice fell flatly, insinuatingly, across the quiet. His friends stirred uncomfortably around the table, avoiding each other's eyes. Albert looked at Olivia, while she stared calmly back at Jimmy, entirely unmoved.

'I don't know what you mean, Jimmy. Ms Belcourt is here because she's the daughter of an old friend.'

Jimmy sniggered briefly. 'That's as may be. But that's not why you sent her such a special invitation. Why you wanted her here tonight, rather than at the grand reopening tomorrow.'

Albert and Olivia were carefully not looking at each other now, saying nothing. Thomas scowled heavily.

'Shut up, Jimmy. You're drunk.'

'No, that's Eileen,' said Jimmy. 'I can still see things clearly. You know exactly what I'm talking about, Olivia. Penny's only here because you need her money. You need her to invest in your precious inn. Just like you needed her father's money, all those years ago.'

No one around the table said anything, but I could feel an undercurrent of anger moving among the four friends. The subject no one wanted to talk about, that had been bubbling under the surface all evening, was finally out in the open. I looked round the table, fascinated. A hidden truth from out of the past was about to be dragged into the light, and I couldn't wait to hear what it was. Penny gave Olivia a hard look.

'What does he mean, Olivia? Why were the two of you so keen to have me here, when you haven't spoken a word to me in twenty years?'

Olivia sighed, and seemed to slump just a little in her chair. Albert patted her reassuringly on the arm, but she didn't even look at him. When Olivia finally answered, her voice was calm, tired, and more than a little guilty.

'Your father was a business associate of ours, as well as an old friend. We consulted with him on various deals to our mutual advantage. Never anything big; I think it amused him to act as our mentor. It was a way for him to make money outside his normal business dealings, and a way for us to raise money without paying ruinous interest to the banks. But twenty years ago, everyone at this table came together in an ambitious scheme: to buy and restore the Castle Inn and run it ourselves. We were all going to do it together because we were such good friends. Those four put in their life savings, as seed money; basically a bribe to the inn's owners not to accept any other offer. That's how local business works sometimes. And then Albert and I went to see your father to persuade him to put up the rest of the money. We'd have paid him back out of the first year's profits. That was the plan that we'd all agreed on.

'But our timing couldn't have been worse. Your father couldn't help us. He was temporarily overextended, and fighting his own board for control of his company. We spent the whole weekend trying to persuade him, but got nowhere. And while we were away, the deal collapsed . . . The Castle's owners got tired of waiting, went with another offer, and refused to return our bribe money. So our four friends lost all the money they'd put in.'

'That's why you had to leave town?' I said.

'Yes,' said Albert, glowering round the table. 'Our friends blamed us for their losses. Even though it wasn't our fault.'

'We couldn't face them, after letting them down,' said Olivia. 'It was better for all of us that we left. But now we're back! We've put all our money into the Castle, and this time it will work.'

'We didn't just lose our savings,' said Jimmy. 'We lost our only real chance to break free from this awful town. To raise enough money to get away and make something of ourselves.'

'Jimmy . . .' said Thomas.

'No, Thomas, it's true,' said Valerie. 'With all of our savings gone, we were trapped here. No hope, no future, no way out.'

'I'm sorry about what happened,' said Olivia. 'You know I am, we both are. But you could still have left Black Rock Towen and taken your chances. Albert and I did.' She turned to face Penny squarely. 'We invited you because we believe Walter would have wanted you to be here. To see us running the Castle and making a success of it. We wanted you here, in his memory. We haven't asked you for money, because we don't need it.'

The tension around the table was slowly fading away. The secret was out, the old grievances had been aired, and it hadn't been so terrible after all. Thomas looked at Jimmy, who was still sulking, and nudged him hard in the side with his elbow.

'Apologize, Jimmy.'

'What for?' he said sullenly. 'Speaking the truth? You know it doesn't matter how much money they've sunk into the Castle. They'll always need more. This place is a money pit, always has been. What are you going to do, Olivia, when the tourists don't arrive in the numbers you need?'

'They'll come,' said Olivia. 'Tyrone's story and the legend of the Castle will bring them streaming in from all over the country.'

'Exactly,' said Albert. 'They won't be able to stay away once they hear what happened here.'

Olivia pushed her chair back and got to her feet. 'You'll have to excuse me. I need to check how the dessert is doing.'

She headed for the side door. Alfred didn't go with her. He

was still glowering at Jimmy, who was pretending an interest in his wine glass so he wouldn't have to look up.

'What are we having for dessert?' I called after Olivia.

'It's a surprise,' she said, not looking back.

She disappeared through the side door and into the kitchen. I surreptitiously sniffed at the air while the door was open, trying to get some clue as to what the dessert might be. But all I picked up was old smells from the dinner, still hanging heavily on the air.

The atmosphere around the table remained somewhat strained. I decided I'd better get the conversation started again if I didn't want to sit in silence for the rest of the evening.

'Albert,' I said, 'do you know why there was only the one tree standing outside the Castle?'

He shook his head, but seemed grateful for the change in subject. 'It never occurred to me to ask. It's just . . . always been there. Until the storm ripped it up by the roots.'

'Was it a part of the old wood?' said Penny. 'The one we passed through on the way here.'

'Nettie's Wood,' said Valerie. 'No, the trees never did come all the way out to the cliffs. The ground is too stony. The old smugglers planted the tree when they built the inn, and did something to keep it alive. Maybe they watered it with the blood of their victims . . . or the good brandy from France. You have to remember, the tree was taken from Nettie's Wood . . . And she was the witch whose voice alone was enough to drive people mad . . . Having one of her trees outside the inn was a ploy by the smugglers to assure the local people that they had Nettie's blessing, and protection. The tree was supposed to have magical attributes, though exactly what depends on which stories you listen to. Most of them agree that on certain nights, when the wind was blowing from Nettie's Wood, you could hear voices whispering among the branches.'

'Do you mean Voices?' said Penny.

'Possibly,' said Valerie.

'Which could explain why the tree keeps coming back, even after being uprooted and destroyed,' said Thomas.

'Have you ever seen it?' I said.

'No,' said Thomas. 'But then I haven't come out here for over twenty years.'

'Do you know anyone who has seen it?' I asked.

'Everyone knows someone who has,' said Eileen. 'It's that kind of story, and that kind of tree.'

'No one's had reason to come out here for ages,' said Thomas. 'So it's no wonder that the sightings have dropped off.'

'If a tree appears and disappears and no one sees it, does it really exist?' said Eileen.

'A ghost tree?' I said.

'It could be a recurring image from the past,' said Thomas. 'Just a little bit of history repeating.'

'You've been reading the *Fortean Times* again,' said Eileen.

'When the tree does make an appearance, does it mean anything?' said Penny. 'Is it significant?'

'No one knows,' said Eileen. 'If the tree should happen to manifest while you're here, you can always go out and ask it.'

'You do, and you're on your own,' said Jimmy.

'I don't believe in ghosts,' I said firmly. 'And I definitely don't believe in spectral trees.'

'Olivia's taking her time in the kitchen,' said Albert. 'I'd better go and see if she needs a hand.'

He pushed his chair back from the table, got to his feet, and went over to the side door. He pushed it open and called out to Olivia. We all sat there and watched him. The moment lengthened, but there was no reply. Albert made an impatient noise and strode through into the kitchen. The door slammed shut behind him.

'Ten to one she's dropped the pudding on the floor,' said Jimmy, 'and is desperately trying to scrape the mess up before anyone notices. I think I'll just ask for the cheese and biscuits.'

There was some laughter around the table, quickly cut off as the side door swung open. Albert stood in the doorway, staring at us.

'Olivia isn't in the kitchen,' he said.

We all looked at each other, and then back at Albert.

'Is there another door?' I said. 'Another way out of the kitchen?'

'No,' said Albert. 'Not even a window.'

'She didn't come back in here,' said Jimmy. 'I would have noticed.'

'She's not in the kitchen!' said Albert, his voice rising. 'There's no sign of her anywhere!'

He left the doorway, hurried down the room to the bar at the far end, and looked up the tucked-away staircase that led to the guest rooms upstairs.

'She didn't go that way, either,' said Jimmy. 'I'd have noticed.'

Albert ignored him, and shouted up the stairs to Olivia. We all sat very still, listening, but again there was no reply. I turned to Penny.

'I'm starting to get a really bad feeling about this.'

'Me too,' said Penny. 'I think our nice normal weekend is over.'

'Let's not panic just yet,' I said. 'There could be any number of reasons why Olivia's not answering.'

'There could,' said Penny. 'But not many good ones.'

Albert turned back to look at us. He seemed genuinely worried. 'Would you all please . . . Would you all just go to the windows and take a look outside? See if she's out there.'

'Oh, come on! How could she have got to the front door without any of us seeing her?' said Jimmy.

'Just do it!' said Albert.

'Better do as he says,' said Thomas, getting to his feet. The rest of us started to push our chairs away from the table.

'Is there a back door somewhere?' Penny asked quietly. 'Could she have left the inn that way?'

'There's only ever been one entrance to the Castle,' said Valerie. 'The smugglers designed it that way.'

'I'm going to check upstairs,' said Albert.

He hurried up the wooden staircase, his feet slamming loudly on the bare steps. We could all hear him calling Olivia's name, over and over again, but there was never any answer. The quiet of the Castle was starting to feel just a little unnerving. We all looked at each other, and there was a real unease in every-one's face.

'Olivia can't have just vanished,' said Jimmy. 'I mean, she can't just have gone without any of us seeing her leave . . .'

'And why would she want to go, anyway?' said Thomas. 'It doesn't make any sense.'

I went over to the side door and pushed it open. The kitchen was a compact little room, all white tiles and modern appliances, with signs of food preparation everywhere. It was quite definitely empty. No door, no window, no way out. I turned back to find everyone staring at me. I shook my head slowly.

'I think we need to take a look out the windows,' said Penny. 'See what there is to see.'

There were three windows in the long stone wall, looking out over the car park. Penny and I took the window nearest the door. Night had fallen while we were eating. It was dark outside now, and with all of the inn's lights blazing behind us it was hard to see anything. Even for me. The wind was blowing really hard. It sounded cold and fierce, not a good night to be outside. I turned to Penny.

'Switch off the lights.'

'What?' said Jimmy. 'Why the hell would we want to do that? I don't want to stand around in the dark . . .'

'Shut up, Jimmy,' said Valerie. 'It'll help us to see out.'

'Do it,' said Thomas.

'Where are the switches?' said Penny.

'By the coat stand, near the front door,' I said. 'I spotted them when we first arrived.'

'Of course you did,' said Penny. 'You would.'

I always make a point of noticing things like that about any room I'm in. You never know when you might need to seize the advantage or make a sudden exit. Penny hurried over to the switches and turned them all off. The lights went out, apart from two set directly over the bar. A heavy gloom fell across the long dining room, and the inn didn't feel nearly as inviting any more. We all looked out the windows again. I could see the car park quite clearly now.

'I can't see Olivia anywhere,' said Thomas. He had his face so close to the window his nose was flattened against the glass. 'Can anyone see her?'

Everyone made negative noises. Eileen was standing very close to Thomas as they stared out through the middle window, and for the first time she didn't have a glass in her hand.

Jimmy and Valerie were huddled together before the far window. Valerie was shaking, and Jimmy had an arm round her shoulders.

'Olivia isn't anywhere in the car park,' I said.

'You've got better eyes than the rest of us if you can see that far!' said Jimmy. 'Can you see the tree?'

'Not funny, Jimmy,' said Thomas.

'Sorry . . .'

We all turned away from the windows as Albert came hurrying back down the stairs. He slammed to a halt at the bottom, started to say something, and then stopped.

'Why are all the lights off? Have the fuses gone?'

'We turned them off so we could see better,' said Thomas. 'Olivia isn't outside, Albert.'

Penny went back to the switches and turned the lights back on. We all winced. The lights seemed almost unbearably harsh now, and not in the least comforting.

'I've checked all the guest rooms upstairs,' said Albert. 'Olivia isn't in any of them.'

'There's nowhere up there she could be hiding?' I said.

'Why would she hide?' Albert said angrily. 'And if she could hear me, she'd answer me! Why don't you . . .' He stopped himself, with an effort. 'Sorry. I'm sorry . . . I looked everywhere. There's nowhere upstairs she could be. Nowhere.'

'She's not outside,' said Thomas.

'Are you sure?' said Albert.

'Come and see for yourself,' said Jimmy.

'There's only one way for us to be sure,' I said. 'We have to go outside and check.'

No one moved. Everyone was looking at me, saying nothing. But I could see the answer in their faces, in their eyes. *This is a bad place. Everybody knows that.* I headed for the front door. Penny was quickly there at my side. And one by one, I heard the others follow reluctantly after me.

The cold outside came as something of a shock after the comfortable warmth of the inn. The wind was blowing really hard, and I had to brace myself to stand against it. Penny clung to my arm with both hands. Darkness had fallen across the car

park. A half moon dropped blue-white moonlight over everything, hiding as much in shadow as it illuminated. Bright electric
light spilled from the Castle's windows and doorway, but
it didn't travel far. I moved slowly out into the car park. Penny
didn't say anything, but I could feel her unease in the strength
of her grip on my arm. The ordinary, everyday car park we'd
arrived in was gone, replaced by a strange new open space
where anything could be hiding. Anything at all. The woods
beyond the car park were just a dark mass at the edge of
my vision; behind me I could hear the sea crashing against
the beach at the foot of the cliffs. I glanced back at the Castle
doorway. The others were standing huddled together in
the doorway, looking out at the night but not willing to venture
any further. Albert had made it to the front of the group,
but that was as much as he could manage. I called back to
him, raising my voice to be heard over the wind.

'Albert! Could Olivia have gone into town for anything?'

He shook his head firmly. 'She wouldn't do that without
telling me. She just wouldn't. And anyway, our car's still
here.'

I looked at the three cars standing together, some distance
away from our hire car. 'Which car is which?'

'I drive a Morris!' Jimmy said loudly.

'Mine is the Range Rover,' said Thomas. 'I mean, mine and
Eileen's.'

'And ours is the Skoda,' said Albert. 'Look, Olivia couldn't
have taken it anyway. I used it last, so I've still got the keys.
She'd know that.'

'Maybe she decided to walk back into town,' said Penny.

Albert looked at her as though she'd gone mad. 'Why on
earth would she want to do that? It's dark, it's cold, and it's
a really long way!'

Penny put her head close to mine. 'It really is very dark,
Ishmael. Do you suppose . . . Could Olivia have heard something out here, come to see what was going on, and then just
. . . stumbled over the cliff edge?'

'I was wondering about that,' I said. 'Stay here.'

It took her a moment before she could bring herself to let
go of my arm. I waited a moment, to be sure she was all right.

Penny glared about her into the dark, her hands clenched into fists, and then nodded quickly for me to go. I strode quickly over to the cliff edge and looked down. There was enough moonlight for me to make out the beach below. There was no sign of a body. I went back to Penny.

'No sign of Olivia anywhere. Nothing to suggest she was ever out here.'

'If she had fallen . . . would we have heard her scream, inside the inn?' said Penny.

'I didn't hear anything,' I said. 'But then I wasn't listening.'

Penny linked her arm through mine. She was shivering. 'At least the tree isn't here. I half expected to come out here and find Olivia hanging from one of the branches. Right next to Elliot Tyrone.'

'A ghost tree?' I said. 'Really?'

'We've seen stranger things!'

She was right. We had. I led her back to the others, still crammed together in the doorway. They looked at me hopefully, but all I could do was shake my head.

'I don't see how Olivia could have come out here without any of us noticing,' I said. 'She has to be inside the Castle, somewhere. We'll just have to search the whole place thoroughly from top to bottom.'

'I've already done that!' said Albert. He was hugging himself tightly now, as though trying to hold himself together. Thomas put an arm across Albert's shoulders.

'Let's go back in and give it another try, eh? A fresh pair of eyes and all that. Don't you worry, Albert, we'll find her. She has to be somewhere.'

Albert shrugged off Thomas's arm and pushed through the others to go back inside. We all followed him in. I took one last look around the empty car park, and tried to convince myself I didn't feel something looking back.

Inside the Castle the bright lights felt warm and cheerful, but that didn't help much. I shut the door firmly against the dark and the night. And then we all just stood around and looked at each other. It was clear none of them knew what to do for the best, so I would have to take charge or nothing would get done. I was just working out who to send where, when Albert's head came up suddenly.

'My phone! Olivia and I keep our phones with us at all times. Because you never know when some business matter might come up that needs to be discussed. Olivia doesn't like me making decisions on my own . . . I'll ring her. Wherever Olivia is, she'll have her phone with her.'

He fished in his jacket pocket, while I thought, but didn't say, 'Even if Olivia doesn't answer, we should still be able to hear the phone ringing and we can track where she is from that.' But Albert was frowning. The phone wasn't in the pocket where he thought it should be. He tried all his pockets, and then looked at us blankly.

'I don't understand. It isn't there. I know I had it earlier . . .'

'Give me Olivia's number,' I said. 'I'll ring her.'

Albert rattled off the number, while I went over to the coat stand by the front door. But the phone wasn't in the jacket pocket where I keep it. I felt a sudden chill, as though I'd put my foot down in the dark for a step that should have been there and wasn't. I always keep my phone in the same pocket, in case the Colonel needs to call me. I checked through all my other pockets, just in case. But it wasn't in any of them, either. I turned back to face the others.

'My phone is gone, too.'

Thomas searched through the pockets of his leather jacket. Eileen, Jimmy and Valerie hurried over to the coat stand. I stepped back to give them room, and they all but fought each other to get to their own coat first. After they'd got their hands on their coats and searched through the pockets, I could tell the answer from the look on their faces. They looked lost, cut off from the world without their phones.

'How is this possible?' said Jimmy.

'What the hell is going on?' said Valerie.

No one had any answer for her. We put our coats back on the rack, as neatly as possible, for want of anything else to do. And then we all went back to our table and sat down again. Perhaps because it was the last place we'd been, when the world still made sense. Some of them looked as if they would collapse if they didn't sit down. I was thinking hard. Olivia disappearing could have been some kind of accident, but all our phones disappearing spoke of planning and preparation. And enemy action.

'We're cut off,' said Jimmy. 'We can't even call for help.'

I looked at Albert. 'Does the Castle have a land line?'

'Yes!' said Albert. 'Of course!'

He jumped to his feet and all but ran the length of the room, to the bar at the far end. He moved in behind it, reached down, and came up with a handset. He lifted the receiver and started to punch in the numbers.

'I'm calling the police!'

I really wasn't comfortable with that, but I couldn't say anything. It was the sensible thing to do. I could always slip away in the confusion. And if there wasn't any confusion, I'd make some. Albert took the receiver away from his ear and stared at it. He shook the receiver hard and listened again. Then he put it down and looked at us.

'There's no dialling tone. The line's dead. What the hell is going on?'

Penny glared at me. 'This was supposed to be a nice normal weekend, but everywhere we go something weird happens! You're a jinx!'

I shrugged. I'd been called worse.

# FOUR

## Who's There?

For a while, no one seemed to want to say anything. We all just sat round the table staring at Albert. He looked at the phone as though it had betrayed him, and then slowly came back to join the rest of us. He sat down heavily and stared blankly at the table top. I looked around the table. Thomas appeared to have shrunk in on himself, all his strength just drained away. Eileen sat close beside him, her face set and stern. Valerie kept looking around her, lost for anything to say or do, as though she couldn't believe what was happening. Jimmy seemed ready to lash out at anything, just to make himself feel better. And Penny was looking at me, waiting for me to explain what the hell was going on.

But I didn't have a clue.

Jimmy slammed his hand down on the table top. 'I say we all get the hell out of here! Right now! Just get in our cars and go!'

There was a brief flurry of nodding heads and loud overlapping agreements, as everyone started to get to their feet. Only to stop where they were, as the look on Jimmy's face changed. He'd thrust one hand into his trouser pocket and was rummaging around increasingly frantically. He stopped and looked at the rest of us.

'My car keys are gone. I always keep them in this pocket. I always . . .'

He searched quickly through his other pockets, but still couldn't find his keys. Albert checked slowly through his trouser pockets, while Eileen nudged Thomas in the ribs and made him check his jacket. Penny looked at me, but I'd already searched all my pockets and come up empty-handed.

'We can't all have lost our car keys . . .' said Eileen.

'They're gone!' said Jimmy. 'Disappeared, like our phones.'

'Like Olivia,' said Albert.

Everyone sat down again. It was obvious we weren't going anywhere.

'This is just insane!' said Thomas, his voice rising querulously. 'None of this makes any sense!'

'I told you this was a bad place,' said Eileen.

'The first thing we need to do, is make sure Olivia really has vanished,' I said. I kept my voice carefully calm, because the others needed to believe someone knew what they were doing. 'All of you stay here, while Penny and I go upstairs and search the guest rooms thoroughly.'

'I already looked,' said Albert.

'We'll look harder,' I said.

Jimmy bristled at me. 'What gives you the right to take charge and order the rest of us around?'

'I used to do private security work,' I said. 'I've spent a lot of time dealing with dangerous situations, which means I'm the most qualified person in this room to keep the rest of you alive.'

'It's true,' said Penny. 'He really is.'

'Then why are you leaving us to go upstairs?' said Thomas.

'Because if there is a secret hiding place anywhere on the next floor, or any evidence that might help to explain Olivia's disappearance, I'll find it,' I said. 'I'm good at finding things other people don't want me to.'

'Who exactly did you do this security work for?' Jimmy said suspiciously.

I looked at him, until he looked away.

'Do you want us to search the ground floor?' said Eileen. 'I'm ready to tear the whole place apart.'

Albert looked at her and seemed about to say something, but didn't.

'Let's not start smashing things up just yet,' I said. 'You never know when we might need something. But by all means take a good look around. There's always the chance something useful will turn up.'

'Like a body?' said Jimmy.

'Jimmy!' said Eileen.

'Somebody had to say it,' said Jimmy.

'No they didn't,' said Eileen. 'Olivia is missing. That's all.'

'The toilet!' Valerie said suddenly. 'We haven't looked in the toilet!' She turned to Albert. 'Where is it?'

He pointed down the room. 'Tucked away under the stairs.'

'How could Olivia have walked the whole length of the room and gone in there without any of us noticing?' said Jimmy.

'I don't know!' said Thomas, rounding angrily on Jimmy. 'But we have to look! What's the matter with you? Don't you want to find Olivia?'

'Of course I do,' said Jimmy, making an effort to control himself in the face of Thomas's rising anger. 'I'm just saying . . .'

'Well don't,' said Eileen.

I thought Jimmy had a point, but I nodded encouragingly to Eileen anyway. 'Start with the toilet, then get Albert to show you every nook and cranny.'

'I don't think Albert is in any condition to make useful suggestions,' Valerie said quietly. 'Look at him. He's in shock.'

'He needs to be doing something,' Eileen said firmly. 'Keeping busy is the best thing for him.'

'He's lost his wife!' said Valerie.

'I know,' said Eileen. 'Some men just can't cope unless there's someone there to tell them what to do.'

She didn't look at her husband, and he didn't look at her. Thomas's lips were moving silently. Perhaps in prayer. I got to my feet and headed for the stairs, with Penny right behind me.

When we got to the staircase Penny made a point of taking the lead, just to make it clear she wasn't frightened of anything. I followed after her, and our feet slammed loudly on the bare wooden steps, warning anyone upstairs that we were coming. We quickly emerged on to a narrow landing, with three closed guest-room doors. There was just the one small window at the end of the landing, and no other obvious way out. I opened each closed door in turn, and then stood back and watched to see if they would swing closed by themselves. They didn't.

Contrary to what Olivia had said, they showed no signs of being badly hung.

I gestured at the nearest open door. 'Do you want to go in first, Penny?'

'After you,' said Penny. 'And don't be afraid to hit anything that moves.'

'Sounds like a plan to me,' I said.

We checked all three guest rooms, one after the other. They were all exactly the same: small, cosy, and comfortably furnished. Each with one window deeply set in the thick outer wall, looking out over the car park. I opened the window in the last room and looked out. There was quite a drop to the ground below. And given how much effort it had taken me to force open the window, it seemed unlikely anyone had tried it recently. I closed the window and looked around the room. The bed had been made up, ready for use, but there was nothing to suggest anyone had slept in it. I sniffed the air carefully.

'I'm getting various toiletries, and soap products from recently laundered bed linen, but the only human scent is from Alfred. Definitely no trace of anyone else, including Olivia.'

'Can't you track where she is by following her scent from the kitchen?' said Penny.

'No,' I said. 'The cooking smells are still so strong that they're burying everything else.'

We went back on to the landing. There was one more door, at the far end, which turned out to be the upstairs toilet. I looked inside, but the room was empty. It was so small there was only just room for the toilet bowl and the wash basin, and there was no window. I closed the door again.

'No *en suite* for the guest rooms, in this day and age?' said Penny. 'The horror, the horror . . .'

'All part of recreating the period, I suppose. The customers will be expecting the full olde-worlde experience . . . There's probably something under the bed for emergencies.'

Penny looked at me. 'Like what?'

'In the old days we used to call such things a shove-under,' I said. 'A china receptacle . . .'

'Oh, ick!' said Penny.

I went back into the first guest room and searched it thoroughly. I looked under the bed and inside the wardrobe. I opened every drawer in the chest of drawers, got down on my hands and knees to examine the bare floorboards, and then stood on a chair to check out the ceiling. I tapped the walls carefully, listening for hollow sounds. Then I did it all again in the other two rooms, while Penny watched from the doorway so as not to get in my way. And then we went back on to the landing again.

'Nothing interesting up here,' said Penny.

'Not that I can see,' I said. 'No one's had a chance to use these rooms yet, and there's nowhere anyone could be hiding.'

'Where do you think Olivia is?' said Penny. 'I mean, she has to be somewhere, doesn't she? What could have happened to her?'

I shook my head. 'I have no idea.'

'It is a bit creepy, isn't it?' said Penny. 'Vanishing suddenly and silently from inside a room with no other exit.'

'It's a mystery,' I said. 'Fortunately, we're really very good when it comes to solving mysteries.'

'But this is something different,' Penny said carefully. 'I mean, from the kind of cases we normally investigate.'

'Yes,' I said. 'It is.'

'Do you think there's anything unnatural going on here?'

'Too soon to tell. But it seems unlikely.'

'I am sorry, Ishmael. If I hadn't insisted we come here for a nice normal weekend away, we wouldn't have got caught up in all this!'

'But then these people would have had no one to help them,' I said.

Penny smiled at me. 'That is so you, sweetie. I'm sorry about the jinx comment, earlier.'

'Story of my life,' I said.

I prowled round all three rooms one last time, hoping I might spot something I'd missed. But the rooms stared innocently back. I'd checked the walls for sliding panels and the ceiling for trapdoors, and done everything but tear up the floorboards. The guest rooms were just rooms.

'This place was built by smugglers,' I said finally. 'I would have expected them to install a few architectural surprises . . . The odd hiding place, or an unexpected exit in case of unwanted visitors.'

'They built the Castle to be their fortress,' said Penny. 'A last redoubt, where they could hold off attackers until help came. You've seen how thick the outer walls are, you couldn't blow a hole through them with a cannon. I suppose they thought that would be enough.'

'But why did they feel the need for a fortress to hide in?' I said. 'What were they so afraid of?'

'Revenue Men?'

'I've been thinking about that,' I said. 'In the end, even these stout walls weren't enough to keep the Revenue Men out. So how did they get in . . .?'

'Are you by any chance doing all this thinking out loud so you can put off going back downstairs?' said Penny. 'Because you don't want to have to tell the others you couldn't find anything?'

'Possibly,' I said. 'But mostly because I can't help feeling I'm missing something. Olivia can't just have vanished into thin air! Someone must have taken her. It couldn't have been one of the other guests, because they were all sitting with us when it happened. Which has to mean we're not alone here. Our kidnapper must be hiding somewhere in the Castle. Presumably, with Olivia.'

'But there isn't anywhere!' said Penny. 'And how could she have been abducted without any kind of struggle or outcry? She just went into the kitchen and never came out again. We should have heard something . . .'

'There was a lot of conversation going on around that table,' I said. 'Even some raised voices on occasion. And it's easy to miss something if you're not listening for it.'

'But where could the kidnapper have taken Olivia?' said Penny. 'There was only the one door and we were all looking at it.'

'I know!' I said.

I strode back into the first guest room and sat down heavily on the edge of the bed. Penny came in and settled down beside me. And we sat quietly together for a while, thinking. I looked around me, scowling. It seemed such an ordinary room. Nothing in the least odd or strange about it. Just an everyday room in a pleasant country inn. Which just happened to have a history of mass murder.

'I still say something unnatural must be going on here,' Penny said finally. 'I mean, think of all the weird stories we've heard tonight.'

'Just stories,' I said. 'Nothing useful in any of them. Nothing I haven't heard before, in other places. Apart from the ghost tree.'

'Trees, ghostly or otherwise, are not noted for their tendency to abduct people,' said Penny. And then she sat up straight. 'No! Wait a minute . . . Abduction! Is that the key word here? Could we be dealing with some form of alien abduction?'

I gave her a long hard look. 'Really? That's where you want to go with this?'

'Why not?' said Penny, bouncing eagerly on the edge of the bed. 'If there's one thing you and I can be sure of, it's that aliens are real. And what's happened here does seem to fit all the criteria for your standard alien abduction. Someone disappearing without a trace under impossible conditions. Missing time, maybe even missing memories . . .'

'You'd know more about that stuff than me,' I said. 'You're the one who reads all those trashy supermarket tabloids.'

'But you're the one who knows what's really going on in the world,' said Penny. 'So talk to me, Ishmael. Do alien abductions really happen?'

'Not really my area of expertise,' I said carefully. 'Even when I was working for Black Heir, cleaning up after alien incursions, I preferred to avoid that whole area because I couldn't risk anyone recognizing my true nature. I've heard things . . . but there are so many stories out there even I don't know what to believe. Are we really taking this idea seriously? You'll be asking the others next whether they've heard about any cattle mutilations in the area.'

'Is that a real thing?' said Penny.

'Well, yes,' I said. 'But it's got nothing to do with aliens.'

'As far as you know.'

'Let's go back downstairs,' I said firmly. 'I don't want to leave them on their own for too long. There's always the chance one of them will panic and do something stupid.'

'You have to have more faith in people,' said Penny.

'No I don't,' I said. 'I've met people . . .'

Down the stairs we went and back into the long open dining room. The others were still sitting round the table. They looked up hopefully as Penny and I came back to join them, but their faces fell when I shook my head. They'd really wanted me to find something upstairs that would explain everything that was going on and put their minds at rest. Jimmy fixed me with a challenging stare.

'All right, Mister I'm the One in Charge . . . What do we do now?'

'Did you search this room thoroughly?' I said. 'Including the toilet?'

'Yes,' said Eileen. 'And we didn't find a damned thing.'

'Except that Albert and Olivia were too cheap to put in male and female toilets,' said Jimmy.

'Jimmy!' said Valerie.

'I'm just saying . . .'

'It was accurate for the period,' said Albert. He didn't look up from staring at the table top.

'It's just one poky little room with no window,' said Eileen. 'Nowhere for anyone to hide.'

'There's nowhere down here Olivia could be,' said Jimmy.

'We've done everything we can do,' I said. 'So I think the best thing for all of us now is to leave the Castle and walk back into town.'

They all sat up straight at that, followed by massed raised voices and much shaking of heads as they competed to make it clear just how much they really didn't like the idea. I waited for them to settle down again. When it became clear they weren't going to, I sat down at the table with them and glared around until everyone took the hint and stopped talking. Penny sat beside me, smiling brightly on one and all.

'What's the problem?' I said.

'Walk a good mile and a half back into town?' said Thomas.

'In the dark? Anyone could sneak out of the woods at any point and pick us off!'

'We'll be perfectly safe as long as we stick together,' I said.

'No we won't!' said Jimmy. 'You've no idea how dark that road gets at night. We don't even have any torches!' He stopped and looked at Albert. 'Do we?'

Albert shook his head, still not looking up. 'And I won't leave here, anyway. Not without my wife. Olivia has to be here somewhere, and I won't go off and leave her.'

His voice was low, but completely inflexible.

'The best way to get your wife back is to bring in some professional help,' I said. 'If we walk back into town, we can alert the local police and they can come back here with professional equipment. Find some real clues.'

'Why are you so keen for us to leave the safety of the inn and put ourselves in danger?' said Jimmy, scowling at me suspiciously.

'I don't know, Jimmy,' said Valerie. 'I don't think I want to stay here. Olivia's gone! Who's to say one of us won't be next? I vote we listen to Ishmael and get the hell out of this awful place while we still can. We're not safe here! None of us!'

'We wouldn't be safe on that road!' said Thomas. He was wringing his hands together, and his eyes had a definite deer-caught-in-the-headlights look.

'We can walk together down the middle of the road,' I said, as reassuringly as I could. 'There should be enough moonlight for us to see where we're going, and we'll be well away from the trees.'

Thomas started to say something, his voice almost incoherent with emotion, and then stopped as Eileen took a firm grip on his arm.

'Look at me, Thomas! Maybe there is a way we can use the cars, after all. Couldn't you hotwire one of them? You used to do that kind of thing all the time back when we were teenagers.'

The others looked away, as though afraid they'd be asked to confirm this. Thomas shrugged unhappily.

'That was a long time ago. Cars have moved on. It's all

computers and centralized security systems now. I wouldn't even know where to start.'

'And anyway,' said Albert, 'I'm not sure I want the police brought into this.'

Everyone turned to look at him. His head came up, and he looked round the table defiantly.

'There's no proof anything criminal has happened. And bad publicity could ruin the business before it even gets started.'

'What's the matter with you, Albert?' said Valerie. 'Your wife is missing! Don't you want her to be found?'

'Of course I do,' said Albert. 'But she just vanished! How are the local police going to react when we tell them that? And you have to understand . . . Olivia and I sank every penny we have into refurbishing the Castle. If this should all turn out to be some kind of misunderstanding, Olivia would be furious to find I'd put it all at risk.'

He looked around the table for support, but didn't get any. As much as everyone hated the idea of walking back in the dark, they liked the idea of staying a lot less.

'All right!' said Albert. 'You win. We'll walk back to town. And you can explain it to Olivia when she turns up again. Get your coats. I'll take a look outside and see how much moonlight we can count on.'

He rose to his feet and stomped off, deliberately not looking back. He yanked open the front door and glared out into the night. The rest of us got up from the table and clustered round the coat stand, sorting out our coats. No one put them on. We were all too busy going through the pockets one more time, on the off chance our phones and car keys might have reappeared. And then Albert screamed.

I looked round sharply. Albert was standing in the open doorway, staring wide-eyed at the car park. He pointed out at the darkness, his whole arm trembling violently.

'It's out there! The tree! The hanging tree is back!'

Nobody moved. Either because they weren't sure they believed him, or because they did. I hurried over to join Albert at the door, with Penny right behind me. Albert filled the doorway, staring disbelievingly out into the night. I had to grab him by the shoulders and haul him back out of the way. He was shaking all over, and the moment he didn't have to look at the night any more he turned away and buried his face in his hands. I stood in the doorway and looked out over the car park. But there was no sign of a tree anywhere. Penny crammed in beside me, peering around eagerly.

'I think it was over there,' she said, pointing off to one side. 'The concrete plaque, I mean.'

'I'm not seeing any tree,' I said. 'Are you?'

'Of course not! There's nothing there.'

'Just checking.'

I closed the front door on the night, then Penny and I went back to join the others. They'd already sat Albert down at the table, saying comforting things while attempting to get some answers out of him. He was shaking and shuddering, trying to talk but unable to get the words out.

'What did you see, exactly?' said Valerie. 'Albert, you need to talk to us. What was it you saw out there?'

'It was the tree,' Albert said finally. His voice was unsteady, and he looked like he'd been hit. Hit hard. 'I saw the hanging tree, right where it was supposed to have stood.'

'Did you see Tyrone hanging from the branches?' said Jimmy. 'Or Olivia?'

'Jimmy!' said Eileen.

'I was just asking . . .' said Jimmy.

'Well don't!' said Valerie.

'There was just the tree,' said Albert. 'The old hanging tree. Huge and dark, standing out against the moonlight. It was horrid . . .'

'It isn't there now,' I said.

'It was!' said Albert.

'Of course it was,' said Thomas. 'If you say you saw it, Albert, we believe you.'

'That settles it,' said Valerie. 'I am not walking back to town. I am not going out into the car park, and I am not leaving this room!'

There was a lot of vigorous nodding around the table. They all looked seriously scared, and the more they took in how badly Albert had been affected by what he'd seen the more scared they looked. I had to do something, before open panic broke out.

'Everyone stay here,' I said. 'Penny, you keep an eye on them. I'm going outside to take a look around.'

'You can't!' Albert said immediately. 'It isn't safe out there!'

'I'm not afraid of ghost trees,' I said.

'I thought you didn't believe in ghosts?' said Jimmy.

'I don't,' I said. 'Which makes me the best choice to go out there, doesn't it?'

Outside in the car park, the wind was blowing viciously hard and the night seemed even colder. But there was still no sign of the infamous hanging tree. The parked cars were just dark shapes, and there was nothing else to see in the wide open space. The woods were a dark and silent presence way off in the distance. Nothing was moving anywhere, and the only sound came from the gusting wind.

I walked over to the concrete plaque set into the ground. I couldn't see it in the uncertain moonlight, but I remembered exactly where it was. I knelt down and located the concrete square by touch, my fingertips rasping over the inscribed lettering. It seemed entirely ordinary, and undistinguished. Nothing to indicate a ghost tree had been standing over it just a moment before. I stood up and looked around me. I couldn't feel any trace of a ghostly presence, or anything that felt like a threat. The car park gave every appearance of being completely deserted. But I still had a strong sense of being watched by unfriendly eyes, though I had no idea where they might be watching from.

I wasn't convinced Albert had actually seen anything. It could have been simple hysteria, from a man already in a state of shock after losing his wife. Or perhaps he only saw what he wanted to see, so he wouldn't have to leave the Castle. But suppose he really did see something . . . Could someone have arranged for him to see it? Did Olivia's abductor want to keep all of us inside the Castle, so we couldn't get to town and spread the alarm before they had a chance to get away? Or could it be they hadn't finished with us yet? It was always possible Olivia hadn't been a specific target, just the first opportunity. Which meant everyone was in danger. As I hurried back to the front door, a gust of wind hit me so hard it almost knocked me off my feet.

Not a fit night to be out, for man or beast.

Back inside, I closed the door firmly and then jammed the wooden coat stand up against it. The rack didn't make that solid a brace, but it made me feel better. The bright light of the dining room was a relief after the obscuring darkness of the car park. Everyone was still sitting round the table. Thomas had an arm across Albert's shoulders and was murmuring reassuringly to him. But it was obvious Albert wasn't listening. He sat very still, his head hanging down, driven inside himself by what the world had done to him. Eileen had a glass of wine in front of her, but wasn't drinking it. Jimmy was scowling, still angry because he couldn't make sense of what was happening, and Valerie didn't know what to do with her hands. Penny looked at me hopefully as I sat down beside her.

'The tree still isn't out there,' I announced to the table. 'And I didn't see anything out of the ordinary.'

'Then why have you barricaded the door?' said Jimmy.

'Just in case,' I said.

'Are you sure there was nothing outside?' said Valerie.

'Not a damned thing,' I said flatly. 'Nothing to stand between us and the way back to town.'

Thomas stirred uneasily in his chair, his arm falling away from Albert. 'Perhaps I should go outside, say a few prayers . . .'

He sounded like he was hoping someone would talk him out of it. Eileen put a hand on his arm.

'You can't go. Who'd look after me?'

'Of course, dear,' said Thomas. 'What was I thinking?'

Jimmy smirked at him. 'I don't see what use a few prayers would be, anyway. Unless you were planning a full-scale exorcism . . .'

'The Church authorities already tried that,' said Eileen. 'It didn't help.' She looked at Thomas. 'You stay here, with me. There's nothing useful you can do outside.'

'Don't worry, dear,' said Thomas, hanging on grimly to the lifeline he'd been offered. 'I won't leave you alone.'

Eileen had chosen her words carefully, to give Thomas a good reason not to go outside. She seemed a lot more in control of herself since she'd stopped drinking.

'We have to do something!' Jimmy said loudly. 'We can't just sit here, waiting to see which of us might disappear next!'

'What do you suggest?' Valerie said sharply. 'Do you want to go out into the car park and see if the tree's waiting there for you?'

Jimmy shot a quick glance at the coat stand holding the door shut and reluctantly subsided.

'Maybe we should just barricade ourselves in here and sit tight until daylight,' he said sullenly. 'Walking back into town wouldn't be as dangerous in broad daylight, when we can all see what's happening.'

'Remain here until morning?' said Thomas. 'Do you really think we'd last that long? It's not even midnight yet!'

He didn't sound like a confident man of the cloth any more. He looked like his faith had taken a hard knock; and without it to lean on, a lot of his strength had deserted him. His black-leather jacket suddenly looked as if he'd borrowed it from someone much bigger.

'If we all just sit here together, looking out for each other, what could happen?' said Eileen.

'You really want to find out?' said Valerie.

'Olivia was only taken because she was on her own,' Eileen said patiently. 'Out of sight of everyone else.'

'I haven't told you everything,' said Albert.

We all turned to look at him. Albert's voice had been quiet, sad, and perhaps just a bit guilty.

'What haven't you told us, Albert?' said Penny.

He forced his head up, so he could look at all of us. 'There are stories about the Castle that no one else knows, going all the way back to the time of the smugglers. Stories of people who visited the Castle and were never seen again. They just disappeared. At first people put it down to the smugglers, but the disappearances continued long after they were gone. No bodies were ever found, no traces of violence . . . They just walked in through the door and never walked out again.'

'I never came across any stories like that,' said Valerie. 'And I've spent a lot of time researching the Castle's history.'

'While the inn was being refurbished,' said Albert, 'Olivia and I discovered a handwritten manuscript. In a hole in a wall that isn't here any longer. We think it was written sometime after Tyrone's crime and was probably intended for publication, to cash in on Tyrone's notoriety. But apparently no one was interested. It was basically just a list of names and dates. The chronicle of a mystery with no answer. The manuscript seemed to suggest the disappearances stopped well before Tyrone's time. And since it wasn't a modern thing, Olivia and I decided not to say anything. We didn't want to scare off people who might want to spend the night here.'

'Did this manuscript offer any explanations as to why all those people disappeared?' said Penny.

'No,' said Albert. 'Nothing.'

'So any of us could disappear . . .' said Valerie.

There was a long pause.

'Look on the bright side,' said Jimmy. 'At least we're not hearing Voices.'

Thomas punched Jimmy on the shoulder, hard enough to make him cry out.

'What was that for?'

'Stop scaring people, Jimmy,' Thomas said harshly.

'All right, all right!' Jimmy massaged his shoulder. 'Lighten up, Thomas.'

But Thomas didn't look like he'd be lightening up any time soon. He seemed almost as much in shock as Albert. And as scared. Eileen took a firm grip on Thomas's hand, and he let her.

'Email!' Jimmy said suddenly. And we all jumped, just a little. Jimmy grinned around the table triumphantly. 'We're not cut off, after all. Albert, you said you had a website. So you must have a computer. We can use it to email the local police and have them send a car to rescue us!'

But Albert was already shaking his head. 'Olivia had a laptop. She kept it in one of the upstairs rooms, which she was using as an office. But the laptop was gone when I went upstairs earlier. I haven't seen it anywhere since.'

'Why didn't you say something?' said Thomas.

'I didn't see the point,' said Albert. 'The laptop had just vanished, like the phones. And Olivia. And the hanging tree . . .'

'OK!' I said loudly. 'I am ready to go on record here as saying ghosts and even ghostly trees are not noted for stealing phones, car keys and laptops.'

'Who knows why things vanish?' said Valerie. 'I'm thinking of the story Thomas told us . . . About the scholar who opened a door between the worlds and let something in. And how that creature might still be with us in our world . . . What if it could open a door in space and pull people through it?'

We all thought about that.

'Why would it want to steal our devices?' said Penny.

'Who knows why a monster from some other place would do anything?' said Valerie.

'But if it could open a door anywhere, then none of us are safe,' said Jimmy. 'It could be here in this room, right now. Watching and listening to us, waiting for its chance . . . And we'd never know until it was far too late.'

Everyone looked round the room, including me. Even though I had no idea what I was looking for. The empty room stared calmly, implacably back. Thomas rose to his feet suddenly.

'I can't stay here. I have to get out of here. I have to get out!'

Eileen was quickly on her feet beside him, talking quietly but insistently, trying to calm him down before he did something stupid. But Thomas wasn't listening. He kicked his chair aside and made a dash for the front door. We all went after him, except Albert, who stayed where he was, lost in his own world. Eileen caught up with Thomas and grabbed him by the arm. He threw her off so violently she lost her balance and fell to the floor. She cried out in pain, but Thomas didn't even glance back. He only had eyes for the door.

I caught up with him and put myself between Thomas and the door. He tried to go round me, not even seeing me except as an obstacle in his path. And when he found he couldn't, he threw a punch at me. He was a big man but slow, and I dodged the blow easily. I caught hold of his arm while he was off balance, twisted it up behind his back, and held him helpless in an arm lock. He tried to break free, and then cried out miserably when he found he couldn't.

'Don't hurt him!' said Eileen. She was having trouble getting to her feet. Penny had to help her.

'Now is not a good time to be losing one's self control,' I said quietly to Thomas. 'Take it easy. Everything's going to be all right.'

'It's not safe in here,' said Thomas. He seemed on the verge of tears.

'It's not safe outside,' said Jimmy, watching from a cautious distance.

'I think we should all go back to the table and sit down,' I said, in my most reasonable voice. 'So we can work out what to do for the best. All right, Thomas?'

He nodded reluctantly. I let go of his arm and stepped back. Thomas took a deep breath.

'Yes. Sorry. You're quite right, of course. Sorry about that. I'm just . . . not good at coping with pressure.'

He went back to the table and sat down, avoiding everyone's gaze. Eileen looked at him, but didn't go after him. Valerie and Jimmy looked at each other but didn't say anything, then went back to the table and sat down together. Eileen looked at me and silently indicated that she'd like a quiet word. I nodded to Penny, and she went and sat down with the others.

'Thomas chose the Church so there would always be someone to tell him what he was supposed to be doing and thinking,' Eileen said bluntly. 'He's always been good with people, but not always so good with himself. He needs something he can lean on when I'm not around. He can be strong and brave for other people, but he can also fall apart really easily when he's out of his depth. I've spent most of my life looking after him.'

'Is that why you drink?' I said.

'No,' said Eileen. 'I like to drink.'

'You're not drinking now.'

'I'm busy now. I'll drink later.'

We shared a small smile, and then went back to the table to sit down with the others. Thomas didn't look at Eileen, but let a hand drift in her direction so she could hold it. I looked round the table. Everyone looked back at me, waiting for me to say something reassuring. Which isn't really what I do best.

'Try not to let what's happened get to you,' I said. 'There's no actual evidence that we're in any danger. We can't even be sure something bad has happened to Olivia. There's no body, no signs of violence . . . She's just missing.'

'That probably sounded more comforting in your head than it did out loud,' said Penny.

'But there's nowhere Olivia could have gone!' said Jimmy. 'She just vanished into thin air!'

'So it's up to us to work out the how and why of it, so we can get her back safely,' I said.

No one seemed particularly convinced. Thomas stared down at his hands, clasped tightly together on top of the table to stop them shaking. Eileen sat as close to him as he'd let her, being strong for both of them. Jimmy looked troubled and truculent, keeping himself angry to keep from being scared. Valerie couldn't sit still, trying to look in all directions at once. Penny was looking at me, confident I would work out what to do for the best.

I was glad one of us felt that way.

Normally when I'm working on a case, at least I've got a body to work with. Someone who's been killed in a certain way, in a specific location. There will be evidence and clues to examine, directions to look in. People to question, about where they were when the murder took place and what they saw and heard. And I can compare testimonies, and work out who's lying or hiding things. But here I had none of these things. All I knew for certain was that no one sitting at the table could be the kidnapper, because they were all with me when Olivia disappeared. So? When in doubt, start asking questions and see where the answers lead. I cleared my throat, and everyone's eyes snapped round to fix on me. I did my best to smile confidently round the table.

'Let me say this again, I do not believe in ghosts and I don't believe most of the weird stories I've heard tonight. And even if I was disposed to believe some of them, there's no evidence indicating they have any connection with anything that's happened here. If it was just Olivia vanishing under mysterious circumstances, then maybe I'd be thinking otherwise. But our phones are gone, along with our car keys and Olivia's laptop, and the Castle's only landline is dead. All of which suggests to me that someone has taken steps to prevent us from leaving. Which in turn suggests that some person kidnapped Olivia for their own reasons.'

I turned to Albert. He looked blankly back at me. I did my best to sound calm and authoritative.

'Do you or Olivia have any enemies? People who might want to hurt you?'

'You mean apart from us?' said Jimmy.

'Shut up, Jimmy,' said Eileen.

Albert was already shaking his head. 'No. And it couldn't be a kidnapping for money, because we don't have any. Every last bit of our lottery win went into renovating the Castle.'

'Who knew you were doing that?'

'Well, everyone,' said Albert. 'We publicized it on our website, Jimmy wrote several pieces about it for the local paper, and then there's all the workmen we brought in . . . We wanted everyone to know. How else were we going to bring in the customers?'

Valerie leaned forward and fixed me with a steady gaze. 'You said someone wants to keep us here. You think we're all potential targets, don't you?'

'It seems likely,' I said. 'Which brings me to my next question. What has everyone here got in common?'

They all looked at each other. I waited patiently.

'We're all old friends,' said Jimmy, 'apart from you two. And you weren't even supposed to be here, Ishmael.'

'We were all invited to this special meal at the Castle . . .' said Valerie. 'We were the only ones to be invited to the pre-opening celebration.'

'Hold it!' said Thomas. His head came up and his eyes were suddenly sharp again as he glared at me. 'You and Penny are the only outsiders. We all know each other, but we don't know you. We don't know anything about you. In fact, everything was fine until you turned up!'

'Told you, Ishmael,' said Penny. 'Jinx!'

'Thomas has a point,' said Jimmy.

'Yes, he does,' said Valerie.

'I'm here because I was invited,' said Penny. 'And Ishmael is with me.'

'And we were both sitting right here with you when Olivia disappeared,' I said.

Thomas subsided, reluctantly. He'd thought he'd found someone he could blame for everything; and now he didn't have a scapegoat after all, the fire had gone out of him again. But Eileen was still looking at me thoughtfully.

'What do you think is going on here, Ishmael?'

'I think we're all in danger,' I said steadily. 'Or there'd be no point in preventing us from leaving. Whoever's behind this still wants something from us.'

'But we're only staying here because Albert saw the hanging tree,' Valerie said slowly.

'Did he?' I said. 'Did he, really?' I turned to Albert. 'Just how clearly did you see this ghost tree?'

He stared back at me defiantly. 'I saw it as clearly as I see you now. It was standing right there, where the plaque in the ground is. A tall tree with wide spreading branches. Clear as day, in the moonlight. It was big and solid, and it looked real as real. But there was something wrong with it. It looked twisted, distorted . . .'

'And you're sure there wasn't anyone hanging from the branches?' said Jimmy.

'Jimmy!' said Eileen.

'It might be relevant!' said Jimmy.

'No,' said Albert. 'I didn't see anyone, just the tree. That was enough. Just looking at it made me feel sick. Like I was seeing something that shouldn't exist.'

'It wasn't there when Penny and I looked out the door,' I said steadily. 'And there was no sign of it anywhere when I went outside.'

'Just like in the stories!' said Valerie. 'The hanging tree comes and goes, and no one knows why. You can't dismiss this, Ishmael, just because it doesn't fit with your comfortable everyday world view. People have been seeing such things and talking about them for centuries. There must be something behind all these stories.'

'Something, perhaps,' I said. 'But has it got anything to do with what's happening here and now? Or is someone just using the old stories for their own purposes?'

'How do we find out?' said Eileen.

Penny looked at Albert. 'What happened to the old manuscript you found? About all the people who went missing in the Castle? Do you still have it? It might contain details that could help us.'

'We burned it,' said Albert.

'You did what?' said Jimmy, his voice rising angrily.

'We didn't want anyone to know about it,' said Albert, not looking at him. 'It might have frightened off the customers.'

'We were having such a nice evening,' said Thomas. His voice was calm enough, but his gaze was worryingly vacant. 'Everything was going so well. Good friends together again. And now it's all spoiled. Everything's gone wrong. We should never have come here. The Castle has always been bad luck for us.'

'This isn't about you, Thomas,' said Albert. 'My wife is missing!'

Thomas didn't say anything. He just sat there staring at nothing.

'We're all quite safe,' I said, 'as long as we stick together.'

'Are we?' said Jimmy. 'Are we, really? If someone, or something, could just grab Olivia without any of us hearing or noticing anything, what's to stop them taking any of us whenever they feel like it?'

'Because I'm here,' I said. 'And I won't let that happen.'

'You didn't save Olivia,' said Albert.

'He wasn't with her,' said Penny.

Valerie suddenly shrieked and jumped to her feet. She pointed at the middle window with a shaking hand, her eyes wide with shock.

'There! At the window! A face looking in at us, and there was something wrong with it!'

We were all on our feet in a moment, looking towards where she was pointing. I hurried over to the window, with Penny right beside me. Everyone else stayed where they were. When I got to the window and looked out, there was no one standing outside. I couldn't see much because of the bright lights behind me. I considered having Penny turn off the lights again, but I didn't think the others' nerves would stand it. I looked back, to see Eileen comforting Thomas, while Jimmy had his arm around Valerie. Albert didn't seem to know what to do. I looked at Valerie.

'What kind of face did you see? Was it a man or a woman?'

'Was it human?' said Jimmy.

'I think so.' Valerie sounded seriously shaken. 'I only saw it for a moment. It could have been a man or a woman, but something about it was wrong . . .'

'Everyone stay put,' I said. 'Don't leave the room, don't go off on your own. Don't do anything . . . Penny and I are going outside to take a look.'

'Damn right!' Penny said briskly. 'You're not leaving me behind this time.'

'You're leaving us on our own?' said Thomas. 'You said you'd protect us!'

'This is me protecting you by going after the facts,' I said. 'We won't be gone long. You'll all be perfectly safe as long as you stick together.'

I strode over to the front door, pulled away the coat stand, and opened the door. A gust of cold wind hit me in the face like a slap. I looked quickly round the car park. It all seemed perfectly still and empty. Penny squeezed into the doorway beside me.

'At least something's happening now,' she said happily. 'I don't see anything. Do you see anything?'

'No,' I said. 'And I can't hear anything in this wind.'

'Do we at least have a plan, darling?'

'See what there is to see, and if anything moves hit it till it doesn't.'

'Good plan,' said Penny.

I led the way out into the car park, leaning forward into the force of the wind. Penny stuck close behind me, using my body as a windbreak. Nothing was moving in the wide open space, and there was nothing to see but the four parked cars. No tree, and very definitely no one standing outside any of the Castle's windows. Penny braved the wind to move beside me, so she could shout in my ear.

'Did you really expect to find anyone out here?'

'Not really,' I said. 'A sudden face at a window? That's a very old trick. The easiest distraction in the world – show your face for a moment and then run away. Guaranteed to make people leave the one place they're safe and go somewhere they aren't. That's why I ordered the others to stay put.'

'You think it was just a distraction?' said Penny.

'Has to be,' I said. 'But from what? When taking Olivia, our kidnapper didn't need anything to hold our attention. Just waited till she was out of sight . . .'

I glared around me. It was so dark there was no point in checking the ground below the windows for footprints, or any other physical evidence. Just as there was no point in circling round the inn looking for our peeping tom. Whoever it was had had plenty of time to disappear by now. The car park stretched away before me, open and empty and entirely unhelpful.

'Are we sure there really was someone at the window?' said Penny. 'No one else saw it. Maybe Valerie was just seeing things. Like Albert and the ghost tree.'

'I find a face at the window easier to believe than a tree that comes and goes,' I said. 'But why risk showing your face when you've gone out of your way to stay hidden and leave no clues?'

'Valerie did say there was something wrong with the face . . .'

'She also said she only saw it for a moment. People under stress see all kinds of things. You know, Penny, I really hate this case. No body, no clues, and our only evidence is people seeing things . . . All I've got to go on is my impression of how trustworthy everyone else is. And taking the measure of people's characters has never been my strong point.'

'Good thing you've got me, then,' said Penny. 'But you're right, nothing that's happened so far seems to make any sense.'

'Apart from the face at the window.'

'Apart from that, yes.'

'There wasn't any story about faces looking in through the window,' I said. 'So at least this is something new.'

'Someone is using the old stories to draw suspicions away from themselves,' said Penny. 'Making people think about stories from the past instead of concentrating on what's going on now.'

'So we wouldn't look for modern-day motivations. But I still can't see why this is happening. What's the point of all this? No one seems to have any reason to kidnap or hurt Olivia. And why go out of their way to keep us here afterwards? To carry off more people? No one here tonight is in any way important or rich. Or anything, really . . . Just ordinary people enjoying a night out.'

'We're not ordinary,' said Penny.

'No,' I said. 'And that's to our advantage. The kidnapper had no way of knowing that people like us, with our background in investigating weird shit, would be here.'

'Maybe none of this has anything to do with the Castle,' said Penny. 'Maybe it's all to do with the guests. Or the smugglers! Some hidden treasure they left behind, which someone uncovered a clue to during the renovations . . .'

I looked at her steadily. 'This is not an episode of Scooby-Doo. And I really don't see how the workmen could have uncovered anything and then kept it to themselves, with Olivia and Albert standing over them all the time.'

'They couldn't be everywhere,' Penny said stubbornly. 'Maybe the kidnapper thinks Olivia knows something about the treasure. And that's why they took her, to interrogate her.'

'Maybe,' I said kindly.

'Or it could turn out to be an alien abduction after all . . . And we're all going to end up probed!'

'I think it's time for us to go back in,' I said. 'If only because I don't trust any of them out of my sight.'

Once we were safely back inside, in the warm and out of the cold, I shut the door firmly and jammed the coat stand back in place again. Not because I thought there was anything outside, but because I didn't want any of the others to be able to leave without my knowing about it. They were all still sitting round the table, studying Penny and me with sharp, questioning eyes. They'd obviously been talking about us while we were gone. Jimmy gestured at the coat stand.

'Making sure we can't leave?'

'Perish the thought,' I said. 'Just making sure no one can get in without us knowing about it.'

'Did you find anyone out there?' said Valerie.

'No,' I said.

'They were there,' Valerie said stubbornly. 'Somebody was out there, in the night. Maybe they can come and go, like the tree . . .'

'Hold it!' I said. 'Where's Thomas?'

'It's all right,' said Eileen. 'He's in the toilet. He wasn't feeling well. It's just his nerves. He'll be out in a minute, when he's feeling more himself again.'

'You shouldn't have let him go!' I said. 'I told all of you to stay here together!'

'You're not our boss!' Jimmy said immediately. 'We don't have to take your orders!'

'You do if you want to stay alive,' I said.

Jimmy started to get to his feet, but Valerie grabbed him by the arm and he sank back down again. Still scowling in my direction.

'I didn't think you wanted Thomas throwing up over everything,' said Eileen. 'There's nothing to worry about, he hasn't left the room. And I haven't taken my eyes off the toilet door since he went in there.'

'We could all see the door to the kitchen when Olivia disappeared,' said Penny. 'It didn't help her.'

'How long has Thomas been gone?' I said.

They all looked at each other, and for the first time I saw signs of concern. Everyone looked at the closed door to the toilet, tucked away under the staircase.

'It has been a while,' said Jimmy.

'It's just a small box of a room,' said Eileen. 'With no other way out, not even a window.'

'Just like the kitchen!' said Albert.

One by one they all rose to their feet. We stood together, staring at the closed toilet door.

'He's probably just too embarrassed to come out,' said Eileen. She marched down the room to the toilet and knocked on the door. 'Thomas? Thomas, it's me. Are you all right in there?'

We all waited, straining our ears against the quiet, but there was no reply. Eileen frowned and knocked again, louder. I went forward to stand beside her. Eileen tried the door handle, but it wouldn't open. I hit the door with my fist, hard enough to make the heavy wooden door jump in its frame.

'Thomas, this is Ishmael. We're worried about you. Either you open this door or I'll smash it in!'

No reply. I hit the door with my shoulder and it sprang open, slamming back against the inner wall to reveal a completely empty room. The light was on and the seat was upright, but apart from that there was nothing to show Thomas had ever been there. Just like the toilet upstairs, the room was tiny: barely big enough to hold the toilet bowl and wash basin. There was nowhere Thomas could have gone. Nowhere. Eileen made a low, shocked noise.

'I swear I didn't take my eyes off the door for a moment . . . Thomas?'

'I'm sorry,' I said. 'He's gone. Just like Olivia.'

I expected tears from her, anger or hysteria, but instead Eileen's mouth flattened into a grim line and she looked at me coldly.

'Then we'll just have to find him, won't we?'

I stepped carefully forward into the room. Two steps and I was standing over the bowl. I tapped on the walls, but they all gave the same flat sound. I stamped on the floor but it was solid stone, and because of the stairs above there was no way out through the ceiling. I checked the inside of the door. It hadn't been locked, just bolted on the inside, and I'd broken the bolt when I smashed the door in. I shook my head slowly. I really hate locked-room murder mysteries. I stepped back out of the room, closed the door, and looked at the others.

Eileen glared at me, refusing to believe there was nothing else I could do. Jimmy was holding Valerie comfortably in his arms, or maybe she was holding him. Albert was sitting down again, as if all the strength had gone out of him. Penny was looking at the toilet as though she couldn't believe what had just happened.

'I thought he was safe,' said Eileen. 'I thought he'd be fine as long as I kept an eye on him.'

'It only takes a moment,' I said. 'Was there any kind of distraction while Penny and I were outside?'

'No, nothing,' said Jimmy. 'We've all just been sitting here. Not even talking much.'

'I didn't hear anything,' said Valerie. 'Did anyone hear anything?'

They all shook their heads. Eileen grabbed my arm and made me turn round to look at her.

'Find him, find my husband.'

'I will,' I said. 'But for now I think we all need to sit down again and talk this through.'

Jimmy laughed suddenly, a sharp bitter sound. 'You always want us to sit down! How is that going to help?'

'Because you'll all feel better sitting down,' I said. 'And we need to rest and conserve our strength if we're going to make it through the night. It's still quite a few hours until dawn.'

Eileen led the way back to the table, her back straight and her head up. She'd lost her husband, but not her self control. We all took our usual seats, then looked at each other for a long moment, hoping one of us had something new to offer. Eileen had a look of grim determination. Jimmy and Valerie sat side by side, holding hands. He looked twitchy, she looked lost. Albert looked like his worst fears had been confirmed. Penny looked shaken. I knew how she felt. One impossible disappearance was bad enough. But a second, from inside a room whose door had been bolted on the inside . . . This wasn't just a mystery, it was an assault on common sense. It simply wasn't possible.

'Are you sure there wasn't anyone out in the car park?' Valerie said finally. 'I really did see someone.'

'Not a trace,' I said.

'Hardly surprising,' said Jimmy. His voice was steady, but I could hear the effort that took. 'They weren't going to hang around after they'd been spotted, were they? And given how fast things are happening around here, they must be pretty damned quick on their feet.' He looked at the middle window and then at me. 'But, just in case that wasn't our kidnapper out there, if it was something else . . . How safe are we in here? How secure is the Castle, really?'

'You've seen the thickness of the outer walls,' said Albert. 'Over two foot thick in places. The smugglers built this inn to be strong enough to hold off any enemy. That's why there's only the one door, to make the place easier to defend.'

'It wasn't enough to stop the Revenue Men getting in and slaughtering most of the smugglers,' said Valerie. 'Their precious fortress wasn't strong enough to save them in the end, was it?'

'You said you used to work in security, Ishmael,' said Jimmy. 'Do you have a gun on you?'

'I don't normally carry weapons,' I said. 'And I really didn't think I'd need one this evening.'

'Terrific!' said Jimmy.

'Are all of you sure you didn't hear anything while we were gone?' said Penny. 'Anything at all?'

'We didn't even hear you moving around outside,' said Valerie. 'And since none of us felt like talking much, it was pretty quiet in here.'

'Quiet as the grave,' said Jimmy.

The others looked at him, but none of them could summon up the strength to reprimand him. He looked almost disappointed.

'The face at the window was a distraction,' I said. 'Designed to get some of us to go outside and investigate. To split up the group and make those who remained more vulnerable to attack.'

'Why didn't they go after you, instead of Thomas?' said Eileen.

'Because Ishmael and I were together,' said Penny. 'And Thomas was on his own. Out of everyone's sight. Like Olivia.'

'So, from now on nobody is to go off on their own for any reason,' I said.

'Poor Thomas!' said Jimmy. 'Caught with his pants down.'

Eileen hit him hard on the shoulder. So did Valerie.

'I was just saying!' said Jimmy, though he seemed a little relieved that things were back to normal where he was concerned. 'Look . . . The supernatural doesn't make plans, it doesn't need distractions. It just does what it does. So I would have to say that it's looking more and more as though people, not ghosts or monsters, are behind all of this.'

'But people couldn't do this!' said Valerie. 'Make people vanish under impossible conditions!'

'They're only impossible until you understand how it was done,' I said. 'Like any magician's trick.'

'Thomas wouldn't have gone quietly,' said Eileen. 'Scared, even panicking, he would still have put up a fight. That's just how he was . . . How he is . . .'

'Exactly!' said Valerie. 'There's no way this could be the work of some ordinary kidnapper, or kidnappers. Thomas would have kicked their arse.' She looked at me defiantly. 'What happened to Olivia freaked Thomas out, but he was no coward.'

'I never said he was,' I said.

'Olivia was a fighter too,' said Albert. 'She would never have gone quietly. She never did anything quietly in her life.'

'I know you don't want it to be anything supernatural, Ishmael,' said Valerie. 'I'm sure such things don't normally enter into your nice, sane security man's world. But I've done enough research into these things to know weird stuff does happen. I'm convinced one of the old stories connected to the Castle must hold the answer to what's happening here. We just have to work out which one . . .'

The irony of the situation was not lost on me. Normally, I'd be the one searching for some kind of clue as to what kind of unnatural thing we were facing.

'Do you think Olivia and Thomas are dead?' said Eileen.

Jimmy and Valerie actually looked relieved that someone else had asked the question, so they didn't have to. Albert sat hunched over, his head hanging down, not taking any part in the conversation. Penny looked at me, to see what I would say.

'I don't believe either of them are dead,' I said carefully. 'If the person behind all of this wanted them dead, they'd have just done the job and left the bodies for us to find. Instead, they went to a great deal of trouble to make Olivia and Thomas disappear without a trace. There must be a reason for that.'

'Yes,' said Jimmy. 'That makes sense. So even if one of us does disappear, that doesn't necessarily mean it's a death sentence. We could still be found and rescued.' He smiled briefly. 'That's a weight off my mind!'

He was jumping to conclusions. But it clearly made him feel better, so I let him.

'Olivia and Thomas disappeared,' Valerie said slowly. 'So did the tree in the car park. The hanging tree. Could there be a connection with that?'

'I would have to see this very special tree for myself before I believed in it,' I said firmly. 'In fact I would need to be able to walk up to it, kick it in the trunk, and maybe even swing on its branches. And even then I might not give it the benefit of the doubt. I don't see any supernatural element in what's happening here. Some person is abducting people in a way we don't yet understand. That's all.'

'None so deaf as those who stick their fingers in their ears . . .' said Jimmy.

'You can't keep dismissing the facts, Ishmael!' said Valerie. 'Just because you don't want to believe in the supernatural. Not when there are so many strange stories connected not just to the Castle but to the whole surrounding area.'

'But they're all bullshit,' said Eileen. 'When did you start believing in the crap we peddle to tourists, Val? You seem very keen to make us believe in a supernatural solution to the disappearances. Why is that?'

'Because it's the only answer that makes sense,' said Valerie. 'Don't blind yourself with limited thinking, Eileen. It's a bigger world than most people realize. They don't let themselves believe, for the sake of a quiet life. But I've done a lot of research into these old stories. I'm writing a book. Remember?'

'You never let us forget,' said Eileen.

Valerie started to say something sharp, but Jimmy cut in quickly to stop her.

'Don't let her get to you, Val. She's just upset over what's happened to Thomas. That's all.'

Valerie's face softened immediately. 'Of course. I'm sorry, Eileen. We're all worried about Thomas, as well as Olivia. But please listen to me. It's only by working out which of the old stories we've become involved in that we can hope to survive what's happening. I've followed a lot of these stories back to their beginnings, and I'm convinced there's something real and solid at the base of most of them. That's why the stories are still being told today. Because they're not just morality tales. They're warnings. To give us information we need, to help us survive contact with something from beyond the fields we know. These stories follow rules that we can use against whatever's after us.'

'I deal in the printed word,' said Jimmy. 'I understand the power of stories. With the right words, you can make people believe anything. But ghost trees that come and go, scholars who make deals with devils and open doors in reality, Voices in the night . . . They can't all be true. And I don't see how any of them tie in with what's happened to us here tonight.'

'I saw a ghost,' said Eileen. 'It didn't speak to me.'

'Thank you. Very helpful, Eileen,' said Jimmy.

'Screw you!' said Eileen, dispassionately.

'Everything that's happened here took place after the Calverts restored the Castle to the way it was back in Tyrone's time,' said Penny. 'They brought the past back to life . . . Could that be the connection we're looking for? Could his murderous meal be the story we should be looking at?'

We all turned to Albert. His head came up, and he pulled himself together long enough to consider the question.

'I don't see anything supernatural in the story of Elliot Tyrone,' he said slowly. 'He just poisoned a whole bunch of people. He didn't make anyone vanish.'

'Apart from his wife and daughters, who were never seen again,' said Valerie. 'And he did say that Voices made him do it. People have been hearing Voices in this area for generations.'

'I think that says more about inbreeding than anything else,' said Jimmy. 'The gene pool around here is so shallow you could go wading in it and not get your socks wet.'

'None of us have heard any Voices,' said Penny. And then she stopped and looked round the table. 'Has anyone . . .?'

'I've heard the wind blowing outside, and that's all,' I said firmly.

Jimmy looked at me oddly. 'You must have really good hearing. I can barely hear the wind at all.'

'I still think the best and safest thing to do is leave the inn and walk back into town,' I said. 'Sound the alarm, get some professional help.'

But Albert was already shaking his head, his mouth set in a stubborn line. 'No. I won't go. Not while Olivia is still here, somewhere. And not while the hanging tree might return. You didn't see it, Ishmael. It looked . . . dangerous.'

'How can a tree be dangerous?' said Jimmy. 'What's it going to do? Topple over on us?'

'You didn't see it!' said Albert.

'I won't leave until we've found Thomas,' Eileen said flatly.

'And I'm not setting foot out that door until someone can tell me what the hell it was I saw outside that window!' said Valerie.

'What she said, only louder,' said Jimmy.

Penny looked thoughtfully at Valerie. 'The face you saw . . . You said there was something wrong about it. How, exactly?'

'I don't know!' said Valerie. 'It was just an impression I got. I only saw it for a moment . . .'

I didn't actually shoot Penny an 'I told you so' look, but we both knew I was thinking it.

'No one's going anywhere until we've figured this out,' said Jimmy. 'If the kidnapper or kidnappers are human, then we have to find them and stop them and get our friends back. And if we've become trapped in supernatural territory . . . then we need to figure out which story we're in, so we can work out what specific information we need to make the bad thing go away.'

I realized Valerie was squirming, just a little, on her chair. She was uncomfortable about something, even if she didn't want to say it.

I wanted to know what was bothering her.

'Is something wrong?' I asked her politely.

She didn't want to answer, but with everyone staring at her she didn't have a choice.

'All right! I need to go to the toilet, but I'm afraid to after what happened to Thomas when he went in there.'

'You could always go outside . . .' said Jimmy.

'I am not going outside!' said Valerie. 'Not even if you hold my hand.'

'Use the toilet,' said Eileen. 'I'll go with you.'

'There isn't enough room for two people in that toilet,' said Valerie. 'And besides, there's a limit to how far our friendship goes.'

'You can leave the door open a crack,' Eileen said patiently. 'I'll stand outside and we can keep talking to each other. That sound all right to you, Ishmael?'

'Go ahead,' I said. 'Don't let me stop you.'

Eileen and Valerie got to their feet and hurried down the room to the toilet under the stairs. The door was still hanging open, just a little, because I'd broken the bolt. Valerie stood before the door for a long moment gathering her courage, and then pushed the door open and walked in. The rest of us watched closely. Valerie pushed the toilet door shut, but not all the way. Her voice rose loudly.

'Look the other way, Eileen! I just know you're looking at me.'

'I'm supposed to be looking at the door,' said Eileen. 'That's the point, remember? What do you care? You can't see me.'

'But I know you're there! Or at least, my bladder does. Please, Eileen . . .'

Eileen sighed heavily. 'All right! I'm now looking the other way. So get on with it! And keep talking, so I know you're still there.'

'Thank you!' said Valerie.

Except Eileen didn't look the other way. She took a couple of loud steps to one side so Valerie could hear her, but kept her gaze fixed firmly on the closed toilet door. I could hear Valerie talking quietly, maintaining in a running commentary. Just for the sake of talking. Eileen put in the odd word or two to assure Valerie she was still there.

I was surprised at how tense I felt. Watching Valerie enter

the toilet had been like watching someone enter the lion's den. It was impossible for anyone to get to her, but that hadn't helped Olivia or Thomas. I turned to Penny, so we could talk quietly.

'Eileen is holding up well,' I said. 'Better than Albert.'

'Albert always depended on Olivia to tell him what he needed to do,' said Penny. 'He's lost without her. Whereas Eileen wore the trousers in her relationship, for all Thomas's motorbike jacket.'

'Oh, you've noticed that have you?' said Jimmy, butting in without any embarrassment. 'It's never been much of a secret. Eileen likes to make out she goes along with what everyone else wants, but somehow that always turns out to be what she wanted to do all along. And Thomas . . . I always thought the whole motorbike and black-leather jacket thing was just compensating. Don't worry. Eileen's not listening, she's concentrating on Valerie. And Albert's lost in his own world, poor bastard.'

He fixed me with a hard stare. 'You're supposed to be the man with security experience, Ishmael. So what are we going to do? We have to do something!'

'You're the one who wanted us all to sit tight until morning,' I said.

'That was fine when just one of us was missing,' said Jimmy. 'But now Thomas has vanished as well, that changes everything. We're all targets now. There must be something practical we can do to defend ourselves! Before we all disappear, or end up like Albert.'

'I can hear you, you know,' said Albert. He raised his head slowly to look at us. 'I'm grieving, not deaf. And . . . I'm scared. If someone could carry off Olivia, they could take any of us.' He looked slowly round the room with dark haunted eyes. 'This was supposed to be our nest egg, our big chance at last, and it's turned on us. I hate this place. Olivia's not coming back. I know it.'

'We don't know anything for sure,' I said.

Albert looked at me. 'Why should we listen to you? I saw you drink that whole bottle of plum brandy. What has that done to your judgement? Why aren't you falling off that chair, or sleeping it off?'

'I have a very high tolerance for booze,' I said. 'And there's nothing like knowing you could disappear at any moment to concentrate the mind wonderfully. I can handle my drink. Just like Eileen.'

'No one can handle their drink like Eileen,' said Jimmy.

'I heard that!' said Eileen, not taking her eyes off the toilet door.

'You were meant to,' said Jimmy.

And then we all fell silent, as the toilet door swung back. Eileen just had time to look away before Valerie came striding out. She nodded quickly to Eileen and hurried back to the table. She planted herself in her old chair, next to Jimmy, and glared around the table in a way that dared anyone to comment on what she'd been doing. Then Eileen came back to join us, saying nothing. We all sat a little more easily, knowing that nothing had happened.

'I could hear all of you too,' said Valerie. 'Jimmy's right, we have to do something. Come on, Jimmy, think of something. You were always the smart one, the one who got us out of trouble in the old days.'

'After he'd got us into it,' said Eileen.

'How do we get ourselves out of this?' said Valerie.

'Whoever is taking us must have a reason,' said Jimmy, scowling hard as he concentrated. 'Or if this is down to something supernatural . . . why did all of this start tonight? There must have been plenty of chances to abduct Olivia or Albert while they were staying here. Or any of the work people. So why is this happening now?'

'Because we're here?' said Eileen.

'Because this evening is all about celebrating Tyrone's murders,' said Valerie. 'That has to be it! We just have to break the connection . . .'

'What if we burn down the whole damned inn?' said Eileen.

There was a pause. We all looked at her. She stared right back at us.

'After we've left the building, of course,' said Eileen.

'What about Olivia and Thomas?' said Jimmy.

'They're gone,' said Eileen. 'Albert can tell himself all the comforting lies he likes, but it won't change anything. Thomas is dead. I can feel it. And if can't save him, all that's left is to avenge him. If we set fire to the inn, that should flush out whoever's hiding here.'

'You know, that might actually work,' said Valerie. 'If there's nothing more to this than just people . . .'

'I still haven't seen any evidence to convince me it's anything else,' I said.

'We are not burning down the Castle,' Albert said firmly. 'I won't allow it. Every penny Olivia and I had is tied up in this building, this business. And unlike you, Eileen, I haven't given up. If Olivia was dead, I'd know it. I'd feel it in my heart. And I don't—'

Then he broke off suddenly and looked around, caught off guard. 'Did any of you hear that?'

We all sat very still, listening hard. I could hear the wind blowing outside, but that was all. I was about to say that when the footsteps began. Slow, steady footsteps, sounding out clearly in the quiet. They seemed to be coming from the far end of the room, down by the bar, even though it was obvious there was no one there. I concentrated, trying to focus on exactly where the footsteps were. But they sounded oddly muffled, as if they were coming to us from some undefined direction. And then they stopped abruptly, between one step and the next.

Albert looked quickly round the table to make sure we'd heard them, and relaxed a little as we all nodded. He sank back in his chair.

'We're not alone here,' he said. 'Something's in this room with us. And it's not human.'

'The footsteps sounded human enough,' said Jimmy.

'No they didn't,' said Valerie. 'They sounded like something that used to be human. There was something . . . wrong about them.'

'Are those the footsteps you heard before, Albert?' said Penny. 'When you were upstairs at night?'

'Exactly the same,' said Albert.

Valerie looked at me triumphantly. 'I told you there was more to this than just kidnappers!'

I didn't say anything. I was thinking hard. She was right,

there had been something wrong about those footsteps. I looked at Albert.

'When you and Olivia were overseeing the renovations, did the workmen ever uncover any hidden doors or passageways? That the smugglers might have used to get around unseen?'

He looked at me scornfully. 'No, nothing. I would have told you if they had. It was one of the first things we asked the workmen to look for. At the beginning we still had hopes of finding some old hidden treasure. But they never found anything.'

'What about hidden cellars?' said Penny.

'The Castle is built on solid stone,' said Albert. 'No cellars, no attic, no hidden rooms. This is just an old inn, not your family's country manor house.'

'There are tales of old hidden tunnels connected to caves in the cliff face,' said Valerie. 'The smugglers are supposed to have used them to transport their goods up off the beach. But no one's ever found them. And not for want of trying.'

Penny shot me a quick 'I told you so' look. I rose above it.

'This inn was built to be secure and solid, to be a fortress,' said Albert. 'I don't think it ever was a storehouse, despite all the stories. That was somewhere else. The Castle was the smugglers' last redoubt, somewhere where they could lock themselves in and hold off the Revenue Men until help arrived.'

'But when the Revenue Men finally came, they did get in,' I said. 'How did that happen, exactly?'

'It wasn't a hidden entrance, if that's what you're thinking,' said Valerie. 'One of the smugglers was a paid informer, who betrayed the others. He opened the door and let the Revenue Men in. It was all written up at the time.'

'But still,' said Penny, 'you have to wonder . . . Why did the smugglers feel the need for a fortress when they could have used the hidden tunnels in the cliff to get away? Was there something else here they were scared of?'

'Never mind that!' said Albert. 'We all heard the footsteps. Something is in this room with us!'

'You've woken up,' said Jimmy.

'Wouldn't you?' said Albert.

'But what do these footsteps mean?' said Valerie. 'What do they signify?'

'And why are we only hearing them now?' said Penny.

'Because someone wanted us to hear them,' I said. 'Our kidnapper decided we needed convincing that something supernatural is going on here. I think someone has been listening to us. That's why I asked about hidden passageways.'

Everyone looked about them, spooked by the thought that someone might have been eavesdropping on our every word.

'I don't think it's that,' Valerie said finally. 'But I do think we're not alone. I know you don't want it to be spirits, Ishmael . . . but there is a definite presence in this room. Can't you feel it?'

'No,' I said.

But everyone else was nodding quickly. Even Penny seemed half convinced.

'I'm not feeling anything,' I said. 'Not a presence, not a spirit, not even a cold draught.'

Valerie looked at me pityingly. 'Some people don't. They're not sensitive to manifestations of the other world.'

I was still trying to come up with an answer that didn't involve me losing my temper and throwing things, when Albert spoke up again. His voice was quiet and sadly reflective.

'Olivia is gone. Thomas is gone. As if something just reached out and snatched them away.'

'Remember the door the scholar opened,' said Valerie, 'to let through a demon that was unseen, perhaps even insubstantial . . .'

'But that was just a Voice in the night speaking evil,' said Penny.

'Maybe it got stronger down the years,' said Valerie.

'Is that the story we're in?' said Jimmy. 'The thing from another place? Is that what's after us?'

'I think it's here with us right now,' said Valerie.

One by one we got to our feet and looked around the empty dining room. I still couldn't see or hear anything, but I could feel the tension rising in everyone else as the idea took hold.

'Everyone move away from the table,' said Valerie, her voice charged with a fierce excitement. 'Form a circle, looking out, and hold hands so it can't separate us!'

In a few moments we were all standing in a tight circle, shoulder to shoulder. Penny held my hand tightly, and Valerie held my other hand really tightly. Everyone was staring silently around, searching desperately for some sign. I could hear their harsh breathing, but that was all. The light in the room was steady and the shadows were still. And then, after a long moment when nothing at all happened, everyone started to relax. One by one we let go of each other's hands, though I almost had to prise mine out of Valerie's. She was still looking around hopefully. Everyone else smiled at each other, half relieved and half embarrassed.

'Whatever it was, it's gone now,' said Valerie.

'Don't sound so disappointed,' said Jimmy. 'I was just one loud noise away from having to change my underwear.'

'I'm not convinced anything was ever here,' I said.

'You really didn't feel anything?' said Penny.

'Did you?' I said.

Penny frowned. 'I'm not sure now. Would you have expected to feel something if there had been something unnatural in the room with us?'

'Yes,' I said. 'And I'm telling you, there wasn't anything here but us.'

'You're the only person in this room who thinks that,' said Jimmy. 'Come on, you heard the footsteps!'

'They were real enough,' I said. 'But that's as far as I'm prepared to go.'

'I think we need to hold a seance,' said Valerie.

We all turned to look at her, and she stared right back at us, entirely calm and assured.

'What?' I said, as politely as I could under the circumstances.

'I think we should try to make contact with the spirit of this place,' said Valerie. 'Open our minds to whatever's here with us.'

'OK,' said Jimmy. 'As really bad ideas go, I would give that one top marks. Come on, Val! Something's already taken two of us, and you want to attract its attention?'

'If that's the only way we can get some answers,' said Valerie. 'I think we're dealing with whatever remains of Elliot Tyrone. Brought back by the recreation of his world. Maybe we can reach out to him and get him to tell us what really happened at that awful Christmas dinner of 1886.'

'I didn't know you were a medium,' said Penny.

'She isn't,' said Eileen. 'She just likes reading about them.'

'I can do this!' said Valerie.

'You want us to sit around in the dark, holding hands, asking "Is anybody there?",' I said. 'Really?'

'Preferably in a way that won't get me hit again . . .' said Jimmy.

'The presence is here,' said Valerie. 'Whatever it is, it wants to speak to us. What have we got to lose?'

'You want me to make a list?' said Jimmy.

Valerie rounded on him. 'I thought you believed in me!'

'I do!' said Jimmy. 'I'm just not sure I believe in this . . . Oh hell, let's do it! I don't suppose it's any stranger than anything else that's been happening.'

'I think it's a marvellous idea,' said Albert. 'Maybe I'll get a chance to speak to Olivia . . .'

'I think you made more sense when you weren't talking,' said Eileen.

But eventually we all ended up sitting round the table again. Holding hands and looking at each other uncertainly.

'Oh, this can only go well . . .' said Jimmy.

'Have faith,' said Valerie. 'And be strong. If we're going to get any answers out of the spirit, we're going to have to be steadfast and resolute.'

'I don't really do that . . .' said Jimmy.

Eileen looked at me. 'You don't believe in ghosts. How do you feel about spirits?'

'Guess,' I said.

'Shall I turn out the lights?' said Penny.

The look on everyone's face made it clear that wasn't a popular idea.

'Everyone hold hands tightly,' said Valerie. 'And don't break the circle for anything.'

She looked round the table to make sure contact had been

made, and then lowered her head and breathed slowly and deeply. We all watched her closely. I've attended a few seances down the years (in my line of work enthusiastic amateurs trying to help are an occupational hazard) and I was interested to see what kind of response Valerie would get. How do you follow unseen footsteps?

'Is there anybody here who would like to speak to us?' said Valerie, in a loud and carrying tone.

'Is this where the Voices come in?' I said.

'Hush!' said Valerie, and Penny kicked my ankle under the table. Valerie frowned, concentrating. 'Is anyone there? One knock for yes, two for no.'

But that was too much for Jimmy. 'Oh, come on! They're hardly going to knock twice, are they? No, I'm not here, leave a message and I'll get back to you! I'm going off this idea, Val.'

'Jimmy!' said Eileen.

'What?' said Jimmy. 'Don't tell me you believe in all this?'

'I don't know,' said Eileen. 'At this point I think I'm ready to try anything. At least this feels like we're doing something.'

'You have to keep an open mind . . .' said Albert.

'That has never struck me as a good idea,' I said. 'You never know what might walk in.'

'Hold it!' said Eileen. 'Can you hear something?'

'Probably just rats in the walls,' said Albert. 'Always a few rats around.'

There was a loud banging noise. Everyone jumped and sat up straight. Penny and Valerie's hands clamped down hard on mine. I looked around quickly, trying to work out where the noise had come from. Nothing had moved or fallen over. There was another loud bang. And another. And then a whole series . . . like a long roll of thunder right there in the room with us. The sounds seemed to be coming from all around, from everywhere and nowhere. And, like the footsteps, there was an odd distance to the sounds, as if they were coming to us from some unimaginable distance . . . I could feel the hackles on the back of my neck rising, like the caress of a ghostly hand. And then the noises stopped, quite abruptly.

We were all breathing hard, and trying to look in every direction at once. Nobody moved in their seats, perhaps because afraid of attracting something's attention. I strained my eyes against the bright lights, and my ears against the quiet. But there was nothing there.

'Is that you, Elliot?' said Valerie. We waited, but there was no response. Valerie tried again. 'Talk to us, Elliot Tyrone. We're ready to listen to whatever you need to tell us. What happened to you all those years ago? What did the Voices say to you to make you murder all those people? They were your friends, your neighbours . . . What happened to your wife and children?'

She broke off as a new noise filled the air. Long, slow dragging sounds, like something heavy being hauled along the dining-room floor. Perhaps it was only my imagination that made it sound like a body being dragged . . .

And then that sound stopped, too.

There was a long pause. 'All very impressive, I'm sure,' said Jimmy. 'But if the lights start going out, I'm leaving. Possibly through a window.'

'It's all just sounds,' I said. 'There's no threat, no real danger. Don't let it get to you. And no, I'm still not feeling any presence.'

'Elliot!' Valerie said loudly. 'Can you hear me? Olivia? Thomas?'

There was a loud clattering, as the coat stand I'd wedged against the door suddenly collapsed. We all jerked round in our seats to look at it, but the coat stand didn't move again and the door didn't open.

'I probably didn't seat it properly after I came back in again,' I said.

We all waited, but there was nothing else. The coat stand had broken the atmosphere, and the moment had passed. We could all feel it. We let go of each other's hands and sat back in our chairs.

'I was sort of hoping the table would tilt back and forth, or rise up in the air,' said Jimmy. 'Or someone would get possessed and turn their head all the way round.'

'You'd have wet yourself,' said Eileen.

'Probably,' said Jimmy.

Valerie glared at him sullenly. 'I thought you believed in me.'

'I believe in you,' said Jimmy. 'Not hocus-pocus.'

Valerie turned her glare on me. 'That was your fault! You undermined everything with your stubborn disbelief. You sabotaged our best chance of getting some answers.'

'At least we're all still here,' Jimmy said diplomatically. 'I could use a drink. Would anyone else like one? Feel free to join me at the bar.'

He looked hopefully at Valerie, but she avoided his gaze. He sighed, rose to his feet, and headed for the far end of the room. One by one, we all went after him. Even Valerie. If only because she didn't want to be left on her own. Jimmy went behind the bar to serve as bartender. He poured himself a large whisky, drank a lot of it and sighed happily. Albert looked at him reproachfully. It was his inn, after all. Jimmy smiled inquiringly at Albert, Elliot and Valerie, to see what they would like to drink. I nodded to Penny to hang back, and we stood close together talking quietly.

'You heard those sounds, didn't you?' said Penny.

'Yes,' I said. 'They were real enough. But didn't it seem to you as if they were coming on cue? As if someone was producing them to feed the atmosphere? None of it was in any way useful or informative. It could all have been the work of our elusive kidnapper or kidnappers, trying to mess with our minds.'

'But why would they need to do that?' said Penny. 'If they can take us whenever they want. From inside rooms with closed doors . . . Isn't that scary enough on its own?'

'Apparently not,' I said.

# FIVE

## Time to Go

We all stood around the bar, but no one seemed to feel like drinking. Jimmy had poured himself another whisky, but put it down on the bar top without even wetting his lips. We all stood clustered together at the bar because none of us could work up the enthusiasm to do anything, or go anywhere else. Things really had deteriorated if even free booze didn't offer any comfort.

'We're not safe in here, but it's not safe to go outside either,' Eileen said finally. She seemed to be thinking out loud, addressing the room in general rather than anyone in particular. 'Stuck between a rock we can't see and a hard place that's hiding from us. So all that's left . . . is to figure out how best to protect ourselves. If we're to make it all the way through the night till morning.'

'You had to say "if", didn't you?' said Jimmy.

'Maybe we should barricade the door and the windows?' said Valerie. 'To make sure nothing can get in from outside.'

'You mean the face at the window?' said Albert. 'If that had wanted to get in, it would have done so by now.'

'Whatever is after us, it clearly prefers to pick its own moment,' I said.

Jimmy scowled down the long room at the front door. 'That wooden coat stand isn't strong enough to keep out anything really determined to force its way in. I suppose we could always push something heavy against the door. Then break up some of the furniture and use the pieces to board up the windows. That's what they always do in horror movies.'

'Though it never seems to help them much in the end,' said Penny.

'No one is smashing up any of my carefully chosen and perfectly matched period furniture,' said Albert, very firmly.

'You have no idea how much time and money it took to get every detail just right.'

Jimmy looked at him incredulously. 'Isn't your life worth more? Isn't ours?'

'But the threat isn't from outside, is it?' I said, cutting in quickly before things could get unpleasant. 'All right, Valerie saw a face at the window. But both disappearances took place inside the inn. The real danger is right here. Our abductor, our enemy, whether it's human or inhuman, has to be somewhere in the Castle with us.'

'But that just isn't possible!' said Eileen. 'There's nowhere they could be.'

'There's nowhere Olivia and Thomas could be,' said Valerie. 'But they must be somewhere. Perhaps on the other side of a demon door . . .'

'Are we really going with that?' said Jimmy. 'A door that can open and close just long enough for a demon to reach through and grab one of us? Does that even sound likely?'

'Doesn't have to be a demon,' I said. 'It could be an alien.'

'Alien abductions,' Penny said wisely. 'Such things do happen. I've read about them in very serious magazines.'

Everyone looked at her, but no one said anything. Jimmy shook his head slowly.

'Great! Something else to worry about.'

Valerie looked at me challengingly. 'You really think an alien is more likely?'

'More likely than a demon, yes,' I said. 'And an alien feels more like something we could fight.'

'Your thoughts are so limited,' said Valerie.

Penny cut in quickly. 'Barricading ourselves in still feels like a really bad idea to me. What if we need to escape in a hurry and then find we can't because we've blocked off all the exits?'

Nobody liked the sound of that. The others looked uneasily at the front door and the three windows, as they realized there was no other way out.

'I am never going to feel safe again,' said Jimmy. 'Even if we do somehow get through this night alive.'

'You had to say "if",' said Valerie.

They shared a small smile.

'We should be safe enough in here,' I said. 'As long as we stick together and stay in plain sight. Our enemy does seem strangely shy, in that no one ever gets taken where we can see what's happening.'

'What if the lights go out?' said Eileen. 'What if someone shuts down the power, like they did the landline? Anything could happen in the dark.'

'Maybe we should all just stop talking for a while,' said Jimmy, just a bit desperately. 'Every time someone opens their mouth, things just sound worse . . . I don't need more things to worry about! My nerves have run off to hide in a corner somewhere, holding hands and crying their eyes out.'

'Would you rather be taken by surprise because we didn't consider all the possibilities?' said Eileen.

'I don't know! Maybe!' Jimmy scowled darkly. 'Let me think about it and I'll get back to you.'

'Olivia and Thomas were taken by surprise,' said Valerie, 'when the demon came for them.' She looked at me. 'Call it a demon. Because of what it does.'

'Someone needs a nice sit down and a time out,' said Eileen.

'Shut up, Eileen!' said Jimmy.

'Albert,' said Penny, cutting in once again, 'do you have any candles? In case the lights go out.'

'Of course,' said Albert. 'They're in the kitchen.'

We all turned to look at the closed kitchen door. It looked calmly back at us. No one made any move towards it. No one wanted to go into a room where someone had already vanished.

'The candles would have to be in the kitchen, wouldn't they?' said Jimmy.

'Look on the bright side . . .' I said.

Jimmy looked at me. 'There's a bright side?'

'There are candles,' I said.

'Still not going in there,' said Jimmy.

'We can all go in together,' I said. 'The demon doesn't seem to like groups. So we go in, grab the candles, and get the hell out again. Albert, lead the way.'

'Why me?' said Albert.

'Because you know where the candles are,' I said.

'And because it's your fault we're all here tonight, anyway,' said Eileen.

'Fair enough,' said Albert.

He headed reluctantly towards the kitchen door. Penny and I went with him, to show solidarity, and the others followed on behind, dragging their feet the whole way.

'Albert,' said Penny. 'What was the dessert?'

'What?' said Albert, not even glancing back, his eyes fixed on the kitchen door. 'What are you talking about?'

'Olivia said she was going into the kitchen to check how the dessert was doing,' said Penny. 'I just wondered what it was.'

'What difference does that make?' said Jimmy, from the rear.

'It could still be cooking in the oven,' said Penny. 'And if it has been in the oven all this time, perhaps we should do something about it. We don't want anything to catch fire, do we?'

'No, we don't,' said Albert, looking back just long enough to glare at Eileen. 'You are not burning down my inn!'

'It was just an idea,' said Eileen. 'I've gone off it.'

'What was the dessert?' asked Penny.

'Nothing we need to worry about,' Albert said testily. 'It was already cooked, just needed to be put in the oven to warm up. Olivia and I had decided on a Tansy pudding – an old delicacy from the smugglers' time.'

'Hold everything!' said Valerie. 'I've read about that. Tansy pudding was made from flowers that we now know to be poisonous!'

'Only in large helpings,' said Albert.

We were all standing before the closed kitchen door. No one seemed in any hurry to open it. Albert looked back at us, apparently glad of an excuse to put off going into the kitchen, but it only took him a moment to decide he really didn't like the look on our faces either. He tried for a reassuring smile, but couldn't quite bring it off. He settled for a condescending smile, to make it clear he knew more than we did.

'Olivia and I checked the ingredients for the tansy pudding very carefully. You were never going to be in any danger. As long as no one pigged out on second helpings. Olivia thought it would make for a nice joke, when we told you afterwards. Our little tribute to what happened at Tyrone's last meal. I suppose it doesn't seem so funny now.'

'No,' said Jimmy. 'It doesn't. Tell me there weren't any more little surprises in what we did eat.'

'Of course not!' said Albert. 'It was all good traditional fare. Come on! Olivia and I ate everything the rest of you did. Remember?'

'But were you planning to eat any of the pudding?' said Eileen.

Albert decided this would be a good time to open the kitchen door. But although he closed his hand around the handle, he couldn't seem to bring himself to turn it. He swallowed hard, trying to summon up his nerve, like a diver perched on the end of a really high board. I moved in beside him and he stepped back quickly, happy to leave it to me. I looked the door over carefully and listened hard; and when I was sure I couldn't see or hear anything worrying, I opened the door and pushed it all the way back. The kitchen was completely empty. I heard Albert utter a loud sound of relief. And then everyone crowded in behind me, peering over my shoulders. I let them all have a good look to assure themselves there was nothing to be scared of, and then I led the way into the kitchen.

Albert immediately strode past me, heading for one particular cupboard. He opened it and brought out box after box of candles. He opened them up and dispensed hand-fuls of slim white candles to everyone. There was no shortage of outstretched hands. The candles didn't seem very big to me. Certainly not big enough to last all the way through the long hours of the night. But I didn't say that out loud. Everyone seemed so much happier now their hands were full of candles.

'Why have you got so many candles, Albert?' said Penny.

'This far out of town, the power supply isn't always reliable,' said Albert. 'And besides, Olivia and I thought candlelight would add to the atmosphere.'

'We're going to need matches, as well,' I said.

'I have matches,' said Albert. 'Lots of matches.'

He reached into the back of the cupboard and brought out

half a dozen boxes. Once again, everyone stuck out their hands. Penny moved in close beside me to murmur in my ear.

'There's nothing in the oven.'

I looked. She was right. The door to the oven was open, and there was nothing on any of the shelves.

'So?' I said quietly.

'There's no tansy pudding in the oven, and no sign of one on any of the work surfaces,' said Penny. 'So where is it?'

'Maybe Olivia was holding it when she was taken,' I said. 'Or maybe our demon fancied a dessert after its meal . . .'

'Don't, Ishmael!' said Penny. 'That's horrid!'

'Can we get out of here now?' Jimmy said loudly. 'We've got everything we came in here for.'

'Do you really think you'll be any safer in the dining room?' said Eileen.

'Yes!' said Jimmy. 'Maybe only by comparison, but still . . .'

I held the door open for everyone as they filed out, clutching their candles and boxes of matches as if they were life jackets. Or lucky charms. The moment they'd all left, I stepped out of the kitchen and closed the door firmly.

'Shouldn't we leave it open,' said Penny, 'so we can see into the room?'

'With the door shut that's one less direction we can be attacked from,' I said. 'One less way the demon can take us by surprise.'

'You have a very suspicious mind, sweetie' said Penny. 'I approve.'

I turned to address the others. They were all standing around uncertainly, not sure what to do with their precious candles now they'd got them.

'We need to set out the candles at regular intervals,' I said. 'Properly spaced, so we can be sure their light will cover all of the dining room. And put the boxes of matches in plain view between them.'

'Why not hold on to the matches ourselves?' Jimmy said immediately, always ready to provide a contrary voice.

'Do you really want to be fumbling in your pockets after the lights have gone out?' I said patiently. 'This way we can get to the matches quickly.'

'You're very good at thinking things through,' said Eileen. 'They must love you in the security business.'

'Oh, they do,' I said. 'Really. You have no idea. Besides . . . what if one of you were to disappear and take your matches with you?'

'There you go again,' said Jimmy. 'You just had to go and spoil the mood, didn't you?'

'It's been that kind of an evening,' I said. 'We're going to separate into two groups. Albert, you stick with me and Penny. We'll start at the front door and work our way back. Eileen, Valerie and Jimmy, you start by the bar. And we'll all meet up in the middle. Spread the candles out, stick together, and don't take your eyes off each other.'

'That's going to make putting out the candles a bit difficult,' said Eileen.

'All right,' I said. 'Everyone put a hand on the shoulder of the person next to you, and don't let go for any reason. That will make things a little awkward, but it's better than suddenly finding out someone isn't with you any more.'

'Every times he speaks, my heart sinks . . .' said Jimmy.

'Shut up, Jimmy!' Valerie said kindly.

'I'm just saying what everyone's thinking,' said Jimmy.

'Yes,' said Eileen. 'But it isn't helping.'

It took a while, but eventually we had candles set out on various surfaces the whole length of the dining room. Standing upright like slim watchful sentinels, ready to be lit at a moment's notice. With boxes of matches set out too, ready to hand. We all came together in the middle of the room, and looked around with a certain satisfaction. Just the presence of so many candles was quietly comforting.

'Let's light them,' said Jimmy. 'Just to be sure they work.'

'They're candles, Jimmy,' said Eileen. 'There's not much that can go wrong with a candle.'

'In this place?' said Jimmy. 'How much would you care to bet on that?'

'How much have you got?' said Eileen.

'We'll light one,' I said. 'Just to reassure ourselves. But only one. We don't know how long they're good for, and we can't risk them burning down before morning. One candle should give us enough light to see what we're doing if the electricity should cut off. And we can use that to light the others.'

'I'll light the one on the bar top,' said Eileen. 'It's furthest from the door and the windows, so there's less chance of a draught blowing it out.'

'I hate having to think this way,' said Valerie. 'Always planning for the worst. It makes me feel so paranoid.'

'It's not paranoia if they really are out to get you,' said Jimmy. 'And something is. Light the candle, Eileen.'

Eileen walked back to the bar, in an entirely businesslike manner. Jimmy and Valerie stuck close to her, each keeping one hand on her shoulders. They crowded together behind the bar and watched closely as Eileen placed a Victorian-period ashtray on the bar top, next to the candle. She took up the box of matches and, with a certain amount of ceremony, removed a single match. She struck it down the side of the box. And nothing happened.

There was a sudden tension in the room. We all stood very still, staring at the match in Eileen's hand with a sense of betrayal. A sudden chill ran through me, at the thought that none of the matches would work. Because our hidden enemy was working against us, even in the smallest of things. Eileen threw the useless match away and took another from the box. She set it carefully against the side of the box and struck it. There was a loud rasp, followed by a soft puff as the end of the match burst into flame. Everyone let out a breath they hadn't realized they'd been holding. Eileen lit the candle and the wick caught immediately, burning with a pleasant yellow light.

Eileen held the candle carefully in one hand and touched the still burning match to the wax base, just long enough for it to melt a little. Then she blew out the match and threw it away. She used the melted wax to stick the base of the candle to the ashtray, to make sure the candle would stand up unsupported, and then stepped back and bowed solemnly to the rest of us.

We all applauded loudly. We were clapping ourselves as much as anything. Pleased that we'd achieved something. We went back to the table and sat down again in our usual places. And it was only then that we let go of each other's shoulders.

'All right,' said Jimmy. 'What do we do now?'

'Can't we take a moment to relax?' said Valerie.

'No,' I said. 'We need to talk this through. Try to understand our situation a little more clearly.' I turned to Eileen. 'That story Thomas told us. About the scholar, the door and the demon . . .'

'You really think there might be something to it?' said Eileen.

'Possibly,' I said. 'Thomas didn't give us any details, like a date or the name of the scholar. Do you know . . .?'

'I never even heard that story until tonight,' said Eileen. 'It came as a complete surprise to me. I didn't even know Thomas had been studying the old Church records. He never said.'

'What about you, Val?' said Jimmy. 'Are you sure you never came across this story in your researches, or anything like it?'

'Positive,' said Valerie. 'It came as a complete surprise to me too. Which is odd . . . It's the perfect cautionary tale, and you'd think a story as dramatic as that would have no trouble finding an audience. Unless, of course, the Church powers of that time made a decision to suppress it.'

Jimmy looked at me. 'Why are you so ready to believe this particular story, when you had no time for the others? And why are you so determined it has to be an alien, rather than a demon?'

'I find this story easier to believe because it offers some kind of explanation as to what's going on here,' I said. 'It has an air of history about it. Even though I'm convinced we don't have the whole story.'

'But you still believe an alien, rather than a demon, is snatching us away one by one?' said Eileen.

'I told you,' I said. 'I don't believe in the supernatural.'

'Tough,' said Valerie. 'It believes in you. And it'll do whatever it wants with you. That's the point of these old stories.'

'Maybe that's why I won't believe in them,' I said. 'I have to believe that no matter what is out there I can still fight back . . . I am the captain of my ship and it's loaded with really big guns.'

'Why does the demon want to abduct people?' said Penny. 'That was never a part of the original story. And why take us one at a time? And only when no one's looking?'

'To scare us,' I said. 'It's playing with us, messing with our minds for its own amusement.'

'Bastard!' said Jimmy.

Penny looked at Valerie. 'The face you saw outside the window . . . You're sure it was human?'

'I think so,' said Valerie. 'It didn't look . . . not human. There was something wrong about it, but I only caught a glimpse and then it was gone.'

We all turned round in our chairs to look at the three windows. There was nothing in them but darkness, and nothing outside but the night.

'We have to do something to protect ourselves!' said Eileen. 'We can't just sit here talking endlessly, waiting to be taken!'

'What do you suggest, vicar's wife?' Jimmy said acidly. 'Hold each other's hands and sing hymns to keep our spirits up? What else can we do? We've already searched the whole inn between us, and a fat lot of good that did.'

'You said there were things in the old stories that could protect us,' said Eileen. 'What sort of things?'

'Well . . .' said Jimmy, a little flustered at being suddenly put on the spot. 'Just the usual. Crucifixes, silver, garlic . . . All the traditional defences against evil. And we don't have any of them, do we?'

Albert turned to Eileen. 'Do you have a crucifix?'

'No,' said Eileen.

'But you're a vicar's wife!' said Jimmy.

'I never let Thomas bring his work home,' said Eileen.

'I have a cross,' said Penny. She undid the top bottoms of her blouse to show us the silver cross hanging on a chain round her neck. Valerie revealed that she had one too, shining brightly against her dark skin. Jimmy was genuinely surprised.

'I never knew . . . You never used to wear one!'

'People change,' said Valerie. She gave me a hard look. 'And I don't want to hear anything from you about believing in the supernatural!'

'I wasn't going to say anything,' I said.

'There's a few cloves of garlic left in the kitchen,' Albert said diffidently. 'You can go and get them, if you want. I'm not going back into that room again.'

There was a general murmur of agreement around the table, even from Penny. Which surprised me. I hadn't felt anything in the kitchen. And if there had been anything, I couldn't help feeling I should have been the one to feel it. I was the one with experience in such matters.

'I don't think we're going to need garlic,' I said. 'It seems highly unlikely that we're up against a vampire.'

'Is there anything else in the old stories, Val?' said Eileen. 'Anything we can use?'

'In a lot of the old tales,' Valerie said slowly, 'if you make the sign of the cross over a door or window that means no evil can enter a house that way. The entrance becomes blessed, and barred to all dark forces.'

'But that only works if you have faith in the symbol,' said Jimmy. 'Right? The sign doesn't have any power in itself.'

'Well, I believe,' said Valerie. 'And come on, Jimmy, you've got a demon after you! Isn't that enough to convince you?'

Jimmy stirred uneasily on his chair, then smiled weakly. 'You think God will accept good intentions?'

'No atheists in hell holes . . .' said Eileen.

'Damn right!' said Albert.

'What about you, Ishmael?' Valerie said pointedly.

'I'll go along,' I said.

'Then let's get started,' said Penny.

We all rose to our feet a little self-consciously. Penny and Valerie held their crucifixes in their hands.

'Everyone stay close together,' I said. 'One hand on the shoulder of the person in front of you, just like before.'

'And we should all make the sign of the cross together,' said Valerie. 'If we make the blessing in unison, that should give it more power.'

I wasn't sure it worked that way, but I didn't say anything. I looked at Eileen and she just shrugged.

'Start at the far end of the room, by the lit candle,' I said. 'Then work our way back down the dining room.'

'Why are you in charge?' said Valerie. 'I'm not even convinced you're taking this seriously.'

'Because Ishmael always has to be the one in charge,' said Jimmy. 'Haven't you noticed?'

'Do you have a better idea?' I said politely to Valerie.

She shrugged, and sniffed loudly. 'I suppose we might as well start at the bar, as anywhere.'

I led the way to the back of the dining room, all of us moving in single file with hands clapped firmly on shoulders. I stopped at the base of the stairs and peered up into the shadows. It all seemed perfectly calm and quiet.

'Maybe we should go upstairs and bless the doors and windows there, too?' said Valerie. 'Just in case.'

'I'm really not keen on leaving the dining room,' Jimmy said immediately. 'Far too many opportunities for us to get separated.'

'The stairway is the only access to the upper floor,' I said. 'If we bless the base of the stairs, that should seal them off. So even if something is up there, it shouldn't be able to come down the stairs to get to us.'

'Come on, Val,' said Eileen. 'Start us off.'

Valerie ran through the correct procedure for making the sign of the cross, just in case it had been a while for some of us. Then she counted us down, and we all blessed the base of the stairs together with our free hands. I didn't feel any change in the atmosphere, but everyone else seemed to relax a little. We blessed the bar next, Jimmy muttering something about the virtues of holy water and holy wine. And then Eileen insisted we make the sign of the cross over the door to the toilet, because that was where Thomas had disappeared. We all went along, making the sign of the cross more fluently now as we got used to the movements. Jimmy's blessing was becoming suspiciously theatrical.

We made our way back down the room, blessing each window as we passed it and then the door to the kitchen, until finally we ended up before the front door. To fortify the only real entrance to the Castle, everyone put a little extra emphasis into their movements. And then Jimmy insisted we bless the coat stand holding the door shut, too. Just to be on the safe side.

Once it was all done and over with, everyone started chatting cheerfully. As though they'd just wrapped the inn in spiritual armour. I didn't say anything, but I did nod to Penny to let go of the shoulder in front of her and back off a way, so we could speak quietly together. The shoulder belonged to Valerie, who was so busy talking loudly about what we'd just achieved that she didn't even notice. Which was not a good sign. Penny looked at me inquiringly.

'If nothing else,' I said, 'it's made them all feel a little better. Which is an achievement in itself.'

'I never asked you before,' said Penny. 'Are you at all religious? Do you believe in . . . anything? Or would that come under your refusal to believe in superstitions?'

'I believe in a higher power,' I said steadily. 'I've seen things, out in the field. On some of the cases I've worked on, I have witnessed higher and lower powers intervening directly in the world.'

'You never talked about this before!' said Penny.

'It's not easy to talk about,' I said. 'You really did have to be there . . . And although I have been involved in such situations, I've never seen anything to make me feel comfortable about what these powers might be. It was all beyond my understanding. I think that might even be the point. So yes, I believe, but I'm just not sure what it is I believe in.'

'How very human of you!' said Penny. 'But still, after all that how can you not accept the existence of the supernatural?'

'Because I'm complicated,' I said.

'That time we took on the vampire, it recoiled from the cross we shoved in its face,' said Penny.

'But did it do that because there was a power in the cross? Or because the vampire believed there was?' I said.

'We all have to believe in something,' said Penny.

Jimmy suddenly realized the two of us weren't with the group, and shot Penny and me a suspicious look. 'What are you two muttering about?'

'Religion,' I said.

That seemed to satisfy everyone. Eileen shot me an understanding vicar's wife's smile. Jimmy looked thoughtfully at the floor.

'Maybe we should draw a pentacle?' he said. 'And then we could all stand inside it for safety.'

'We should draw it round the table,' said Albert, 'then at least we could sit down.'

'I think that kind of thing's mostly for summoning demons,' said Valerie. 'Don't we have enough problems as it is?'

'And shouldn't it be a pentagram, anyway?' said Eileen.

'I never was any good at maths,' said Jimmy.

'They're the same thing,' I said. 'A five-pointed star-shaped figure.'

'How do you know that, Mister I Don't Believe in the Supernatural?' said Jimmy, immediately suspicious again.

'I read about it,' I said. 'Dennis Wheatley knew what he was talking about.'

'We could always draw a simple protective circle,' said Albert, 'if you think that would help.'

'You have to add the right signs and words of power to give the circle strength,' said Valerie. 'And I didn't bring my books with me.'

'I think we should just go back to the table and sit down,' I said. 'We've all been through a lot, and we need to preserve our strength and pace ourselves.'

'Besides, discussions always go better sitting down,' said Penny. 'Everyone knows that.'

Everyone liked that idea. So we all trooped back to the table, hands on shoulders, and sat down again. People took their hands away from each other with a certain reluctance, and then relaxed a little when nothing bad happened. The things we'll put our faith in when we're scared enough . . .

'Personally, I'm getting just a bit tired of all this togetherness stuff,' said Eileen. 'I do not usually go in for all this touchy-feely crap.'

Jimmy smiled. 'I can remember a time when you did.'

Eileen stared him down with magnificent scorn. 'Some of us grew up.'

'You want to feel safe, don't you?' said Valerie.

'It'll take more than a hand on my shoulder to make me feel safe in this shit hole,' said Eileen.

'Hey!' said Albert.

'Shut up, Albert!' said Valerie.

'Maybe we should all tie ourselves together with lengths of rope,' said Jimmy. 'Like mountaineers in dangerous territory. So that whatever happens we can't be torn away from the group. Or at least not without anyone noticing.'

'You really think a bit of rope would be enough to stop a demon that can open doors in space?' said Eileen.

'It must have limitations,' Jimmy said stubbornly. 'Or we'd all have been taken by now.'

'I think being tied together could prove dangerously restrictive if we need to react quickly,' I said. 'It would be too easy to get tangled up with each other.'

'Are you really planning on fighting a demon?' said Eileen.

'Wouldn't be the first time,' I said. 'No one is taking me without a struggle. And I won't let any of you be taken without throwing everything I've got in its path.'

'By all means!' said Jimmy. 'You do that. We'll all speak very kindly of you after you're gone.'

'We don't need ropes,' I said. 'Just sitting here and keeping an eye on each other, and on our surroundings, should be enough to keep us safe.'

'I don't have any ropes, anyway,' said Albert.

'We could improvise something,' Jimmy said stubbornly.

'Let it go, Jimmy,' said Valerie.

Jimmy sat and sulked for a while, and then scowled at the old-fashioned clock on the opposite wall.

'It's hours till morning . . . How are we supposed to pass the time? Anyone got a pack of cards on them?'

'Who brings cards to a restaurant?' said Valerie. 'Oh, sorry! I forgot who I was talking to . . .'

'I don't approve of gambling,' said Eileen. 'It destroys lives.'

'Don't be such a wet blanket, Eileen,' said Valerie. 'I play the lottery every week. You never know.'

'Statistically speaking, you stand a better chance of being struck by lightning than winning anything worth having,' said Eileen.

Jimmy winced. 'Thanks a whole bunch. Now I've got something else to worry about.'

'I really don't see us being struck by lightning inside an inn,' Penny said kindly.

'You sure about that?' said Jimmy. 'Given everything else that's happened so far this evening?'

'Yes,' I said. 'Though I could always improvise a lightning conductor and strap it to you, if you like.'

'I think I'll pass,' said Jimmy.

'I still don't approve of games of chance,' said Eileen.

'All right!' said Jimmy. 'No cards, I get it! You suggest something. And don't suggest prayer, unless you like being struck severely about the head and shoulders. I don't believe anyone's listening. Except possibly the demon.'

Eileen turned to Albert. 'You must have something. Pubs always have a few games on hand.'

'This is an upmarket themed restaurant,' Albert said coldly. 'Not a pub.'

'And because it's a period setting, I'm guessing you don't have a television anywhere, or even a radio,' said Valerie.

'Exactly,' said Albert. 'The whole point of coming to the Castle was so people could get away from the modern world.'

'Not a good thing to be pointing out right now,' said Jimmy.

'We could always play word games,' said Penny.

'Not really in the mood,' said Valerie.

'Maybe we should have some more drinks,' said Jimmy.

'Really not in the mood,' said Eileen.

Jimmy cocked an eyebrow at her. 'That's not like you.'

She stared back at him unflinchingly. 'You don't know me, Jimmy. And you never did.'

'Given that you married Thomas, clearly not,' said Jimmy.

'I don't think we should drink any more,' said Valerie. 'I don't like the idea of being drunk and helpless if something was to happen . . .'

'Being sober didn't help the others,' said Jimmy.

Albert looked at me. 'And some of us, it turns out, aren't affected by alcohol at all. Even when they drink a whole bottle.'

'Oh, let it go, Albert!' said Eileen. 'How expensive was that plum brandy, that you're still going on about it?'

Albert looked away, pretending he hadn't heard her.

'I suppose we could just talk . . .' said Penny.

Everyone looked at each other. They weren't actually

opposed to the idea, but no one wanted to go first. Either because they didn't have anything to say or because they didn't want to say out loud what was bothering them. In the end, Valerie cleared her throat reluctantly.

'I always thought I'd be stronger than this if I ever ran into something that was genuinely out of the ordinary. Braver, anyway. After all the weird stories I've investigated, I always thought that if I was lucky enough to become involved in a supernatural event I'd be fascinated. Intrigued. That I'd jump right in and get involved. Study what was going on and try to understand it. But instead . . . all I am is scared. Horribly scared. I just want it all to go away. I want my life back. My ordinary, boring, sane and sensible life.'

'We're all scared, Val,' said Jimmy. He was trying to sound comforting, but I don't think he'd had a lot of practice. He gave Valerie his best reassuring smile. 'It's only natural. We're out of our depth and there are sharks in the water. But you can't let it get to you. That's what the demon wants.'

'It's playing with us,' said Eileen. 'Savouring our suffering.'

Jimmy looked at her. 'You think it's doing all this just for the fun of it?'

'Who knows why demons do anything?' said Eileen.

'It was fun when I thought they were just stories,' said Valerie. Her gaze was far away, as though she hadn't heard a word anyone else had said. She could just have been talking aloud. 'I enjoyed believing in the possibility of strange and uncanny things. Unknown creatures and unnatural events. Ghosts and monsters, and all the mysteries no one can explain. It made the world seem a much larger and more interesting place. But now here I am, face to face with something out of the unknown, and it just makes me feel so small and helpless . . . Like when I was just a child, huddled under my bedclothes at night afraid of the dark.'

'Yes . . .' said Eileen. 'The dark and what might be in it. When I was a child – and I was braver than most – I was afraid of the dark for a lot longer than anyone else I knew. Sometimes I would sit up in bed into the early hours of the morning, reading a book with a torch so my parents wouldn't know . . . Waiting for it to be light enough, so I could finally get to sleep.'

She suddenly looked tired, and beaten down by the weight of old fears she thought she'd left behind her.

'I was never afraid of the dark,' Jimmy said stoutly. 'I always felt it should be afraid of me. If a bogeyman had crept out from under my bed, I'd have clubbed him to death with my cricket bat. But I know what you mean. This whole supernatural thing creeps me out. Once you accept that one unnatural thing is possible, where do you draw the line? Does the existence of one bad thing mean that all of them are equally possible? Because there's a demon, do I have to believe in ghosts and werewolves and the living dead? Where do you stop?'

'Just because we don't understand what's going on, that doesn't mean there isn't a rational explanation,' I said firmly.

Valerie slammed a hand down on the table, hard enough to send it rocking. 'Stop fighting it, Ishmael! Your blind refusal to believe in anything outside your usual comfort zone won't save you!'

'I'm always ready to believe,' I said steadily. 'I'm just not sure exactly what it is I'm supposed to believe here. The ghost of a tree? Or Tyrone's Voices? A demon? Or an alien from some old story? I need to know what we're up against so I can fight it. And for that, I need proof.'

'The supernatural doesn't do proof, as a rule,' said Valerie. 'By definition it's outside our knowledge, beyond what we know and can hope to understand. I think that's probably the point. You have to have faith.'

'There could still be a rational explanation for everything that's happened here tonight,' I said.

'Like what?' said Jimmy.

'I'm working on it,' I said.

'This place is cursed!' said Albert.

Something in his voice brought our attention back to him. He was sitting slumped in his chair, staring at nothing. His face was blank, his mouth was slack, and his gaze was empty. As if the strength he'd somehow managed to claw back after losing Olivia had finally run out, his precarious grasp on sanity shattered by the unyielding facts of his wife's disappearance and his friend's.

'What do you mean, Albert?' Valerie said carefully.

'The Castle, this whole area . . . They're just bad, no good for anyone.' He shook his head slowly. 'Olivia and I should never have come back from London. We should have known better. This place . . . it doesn't want us here. We're not welcome. Just more meat to the grinder. Nothing good has ever come out of the Castle.'

He stopped talking. We waited, but he had nothing more to say.

'OK . . .' said Jimmy. 'Albert's gone again, poor bastard. There's a part of me that envies him. I think I'd quite like to be so out of it that I don't know how much danger I am in.'

'Then have another drink,' said Eileen.

'Not funny, Eileen,' said Valerie.

'It wasn't meant to be,' said Eileen.

'I'm worried about what will happen next,' I said.

Everyone turned their attention away from Albert to study me warily.

'How do you mean?' said Valerie.

'Think about it,' I said. 'If we all stay together in one place, in the light, and refuse to be separated or distracted or tempted into going off on our own . . . What will the demon do next? What can it do?'

'It might just give up on us as a bad job,' said Jimmy. 'If it can only take us when we're on our own or out of sight and we don't give it that opportunity . . . What reason would it have to stick around?'

'You think it might get bored and just leave?' said Eileen.

'Nothing's happened for quite a while,' said Penny. 'Because we haven't given it a chance to do anything.'

'Or maybe the demon only wanted two people,' said Jimmy. 'Maybe it's not hungry any more.'

'Jimmy!' said Valerie.

'No, you don't get it,' said Jimmy. 'If that's it, if the demon is full . . . then all of this is over.'

'It doesn't feel like the threat is over,' I said.

'It isn't,' said Albert.

We all turned to look at him. His gaze was still worryingly empty, his voice flat, almost lifeless.

'Can't you feel it?' he said. 'We're not alone. We're being watched.'

We all stared around us. There was no one else in the dining room. The light was bright and steady, everything was still and quiet, and there was nothing threatening anywhere. But Albert was right, we weren't alone. We could all feel it.

'As long as the demon is only *watching* us, I don't give a shit,' Jimmy said loudly. He didn't sound particularly convincing.

'I hate this,' said Valerie, her voice trembling. 'The waiting . . . Knowing something bad is going to happen, but not what. Or who it will happen to. I almost want something to happen, just to get it over with.'

Jimmy put his hand on top of hers and squeezed it reassuringly. 'No you don't, Val. It's just your nerves talking. Be strong. You have it in you, I know you do.'

She smiled at him tiredly. 'You've always had faith in me, Jimmy. I never know why.'

'Of course you do,' said Jimmy.

'I'd say, get a room,' said Eileen. 'But I wouldn't go upstairs if you put a gun to my head.'

'Dear Eileen,' said Jimmy. 'Typical vicar's wife. Irrelevant morality for all occasions . . .'

'Screw you!' said Eileen.

'Why don't you have a drink?' said Jimmy.

'Stop it, Jimmy!' said Valerie. 'That's just mean.'

'She started it,' said Jimmy.

'It's been quiet for a long time now,' said Penny, deliberately cutting across the argument before it could go anywhere really unpleasant. 'What do you think will happen next, Ishmael?'

'Some new attempt to distract us,' I said. 'The demon needs to do something dramatic to panic us, break us up. We've had the face at the window and noises from nowhere . . . The demon knows it won't catch us with the same trick twice.' I looked around the table. 'Whatever happens . . . we can't let ourselves be pressured into doing something stupid or dangerous.'

'Not much else left to us,' said Jimmy.

I stood up and glared around me. 'I know you're there, demon! Watching and listening. If you want me, you're going to have to come and get me. You're going to have to show yourself, you cowardly piece of shit!'

'Please don't taunt the insanely powerful demon thing,' said Jimmy. 'Isn't it mad enough at us already? Why would you want to see it, anyway?'

I sat down again. 'So I can hit it. Hard.'

'Well, lots of points for courage, not to mention ambition,' said Jimmy. 'But I think I'll hide behind something big and solid while you do it.'

'Room for two?' said Valerie.

'Always,' said Jimmy.

We sat at our table for some time, stiff and tense, trying to look in all directions at once, but nothing happened. And then Albert suddenly stood up. Jimmy actually cried out with shock. One minute Albert was sitting slumped in his chair, lost to the world. The next, he was up on his feet, smiling broadly.

'I've just thought of something!' he said happily. 'I can't believe I forgot all about it.'

'You nearly gave me a coronary!' said Jimmy. 'What's so important?'

'It's in the kitchen,' said Albert. 'I just remembered. Stay where you are, I won't be a moment.'

He headed for the closed kitchen door. We all rose quickly to our feet, calling out for him to stop.

'This really isn't a good idea, Albert!' said Eileen.

'Don't go off on your own,' I said. 'Wait a minute, I'll come with you.'

'It's all right,' Albert said over his shoulder, not looking back. 'I should have thought of this before.'

'You can't go in there on your own, Albert,' I said. 'It's not safe.'

But he'd already pushed the door open. 'This is my kitchen. I don't need my hand held.'

'At least leave the door open, so we can all see you,' said Penny. 'And keep talking to us!'

By now I was on my feet and going after Albert, but he strode into the kitchen and slammed the door shut before I could get there. I grabbed hold of the handle, but the door was locked. I rattled the door hard. But it wouldn't budge.

'Albert!' I said, through the door. 'Talk to me!'

There was no response. The others quickly caught up with me, crowding together before the closed door.

'He locked it?' said Jimmy. 'Why would the stupid bastard lock it?'

'Whatever's in there must be really important,' said Valerie.

'What could be so important,' said Eileen, 'that he'd go off on his own into the room that took his wife away?'

I hit the door with my shoulder and it sprang open, tearing the lock off the door jamb. I stood in the doorway, looking at a completely empty kitchen. The babble of voices behind me shut off. Albert was gone. I quickly looked back over my shoulder to make sure everyone else was still there, in case Albert's disappearance was also a distraction. But they were all staring at the empty kitchen with wide, disbelieving eyes. Unable to believe they'd lost someone else so quickly and so easily.

'Everyone put a hand on someone else's shoulder,' I said tersely. 'Don't argue, just do it! And don't let go for anything.'

They all did as they were told. Without arguing for once, because they were in shock. Penny's hand settled on to my shoulder and squeezed it reassuringly.

'Keep an eye on the dining room for me, Penny,' I said. 'I have to check out the kitchen, and I don't want anyone sneaking up on any of us from behind.'

'I'm on it,' said Penny.

'Albert was right,' Valerie said quietly. 'He and Olivia should never have come back from London. They were safe there. Now this awful place has destroyed both of them. Nothing good has ever come out of the Castle.'

'At least we're still here,' said Jimmy.

'Thomas isn't,' said Eileen.

'Why would Albert do something so insane?' said Valerie.

'Maybe he heard Voices,' said Jimmy. 'Like Tyrone.'

'Wouldn't he have said something,' said Eileen, 'if he started hearing Voices in his head?'

'Would you?' said Jimmy.

'Maybe that's why he was quiet for so long,' said Penny. 'He wasn't listening to us because he was listening to someone, or something, else.'

'Oh God!' said Valerie.

'I don't want to hear Voices,' said Jimmy. 'I'm having enough trouble coping with what's going on in my head as it is.'

'Shut up, Jimmy!' Eileen said kindly.

'Can you see anything different about the kitchen, Ishmael?' said Valerie.

'Not yet,' I said. 'I'm going in. You all stay put while I have a good look round.'

'Damn right I'm staying put!' said Jimmy. 'You couldn't get me into that room if you pointed a gun at my nads.'

'Penny?' I said. 'Anything happening in the dining room?'

'All clear!' she said loudly.

'Wait a minute, wait a minute!' said Eileen. 'I've just realized something. The blessing we put on the kitchen door didn't work!'

'What?' said Jimmy. 'Oh . . . yes. We all made the sign of the cross over the door, didn't we? Does that mean none of our blessings did any good?'

'Not necessarily,' said Valerie. 'All the blessings are designed to do is keep evil out. Not stop one of us from going to meet it.'

'That's something, I suppose,' said Eileen.

I moved slowly forward into the kitchen. Everything was still, and almost defiantly peaceful. Staring back at me with calm normality. There was no sign of Albert anywhere, and no trace of any struggle. Something must have taken him the moment he closed the door. He'd been suddenly and silently carried away with eerie efficiency, as if something had been waiting for him.

I opened all the cupboards and rummaged through the contents. I opened all the drawers and even peered inside the oven. I wasn't sure what I was looking for. Whatever it was, I didn't find it. I dragged the fittings away from the walls so I could look behind them. A few resisted and I lost my temper. I hauled them away from the walls by brute force, not caring how much I damaged them in the process. Blank grey stone and cracked plaster stared calmly back at me. I tore the fittings apart with my bare hands as if they were made of cardboard. I smashed the work surfaces with my fists and threw the pieces around. I raged back and forth across the kitchen, making loud noises that didn't even make sense to me, wrecking everything I could get my hands on. Just to make myself feel better.

I was revealing my more than human strength to the others watching from the doorway, but I didn't give a damn.

That thought was finally enough to shock me sane again, and I lurched to a halt in the middle of the kitchen, breathing hard. More from the force of my emotions than anything else. I wasn't used to feeling helpless, stupid and beaten. I glanced at the shocked faces in the doorway. They looked scared of me.

I took in the mess I'd made of the kitchen and didn't blame them. In just a few moments I'd reduced a kitchen full of the very latest appliances to nothing more than wreckage and debris. Even the electric oven was lying on its side on the floor, torn out of its setting. Good thing it hadn't been gas. A single piece of jagged wood protruded from one wall like a spear. I nodded jerkily to the others and gave them my best reassuring smile.

'Sorry,' I said. 'I lost it there, for a moment. But I'm back in control now. Everything's fine. Really.'

No one said anything. They didn't appear convinced. It was possible my smile hadn't been as reassuring as I'd hoped. The only one who didn't look frightened was Penny. She looked disappointed in me.

'Everyone, go back into the dining room,' I said. 'There's nothing to see here.'

'Not now there isn't!' said Jimmy.

Valerie took him by the arm. 'Really not the moment, Jimmy . . .'

'What are you, Ishmael?' said Eileen. 'Really?'

'Seriously upset,' I said. 'Go back to the table and sit down. Single file, hands on shoulders. Off you go.'

Valerie, Eileen and Jimmy moved away, sticking close together, muttering agitatedly under their breath. They didn't look back at me once. Penny stayed in the doorway, looking me over carefully.

'Are you all right, Ishmael?'

'Not really,' I said. 'I stayed on to protect these people but don't seem to be making too good a job of it. I should never have allowed Albert to come in here on his own.'

'He didn't give you a chance to stop him,' said Penny. 'It was almost like he wanted to be taken.'

'Maybe he really was hearing Voices,' I said.

'Come back into the dining room, sweetie,' said Penny. 'There's nothing more you can do here.'

I looked around the ruined kitchen. 'Doesn't look like it,' I said.

Penny stepped cautiously forward into the kitchen and took me by the hand. Her grip was reassuringly strong, to make it clear nothing and no one would ever take me away from her. She led me back to the table in the dining room and we sat down facing the others. All of us were back in our usual seats, except some of them were empty now. Jimmy, Valerie and Eileen looked at me watchfully, but said nothing. And then Jimmy pushed back his chair and peered under the table. He quickly re-emerged, and smiled weakly round the table.

'Just thought I'd check. I mean, we've looked everywhere else.'

'Bogeymen usually hide under the bed,' said Eileen.

'You're just mad because you didn't think of it,' said Jimmy.

Eileen surprised me then, with a brief bark of laughter.

'We have to talk this through,' said Penny. 'People can't just vanish into thin air. They must go somewhere.'

'But if the demon can open doors in space . . .' said Valerie.

Jimmy rounded on her. 'Will you listen to yourself! Do you really believe what you're saying?'

'At least it's an explanation,' said Valerie.

'Is it?' said Eileen.

Valerie slumped in her chair. 'I don't know what to believe any more. But we have to believe in something.'

'If the demon, or alien, is powerful enough to open a door in reality itself,' I said, 'why do people only disappear when we can't see what's happening?'

'Because if we could see what was going on, we'd see how

it was done,' said Penny. 'And then we'd know something the demon doesn't want us to know.'

'Exactly,' I said. 'Which sounds a lot like human planning to me.'

'Are we really back to that?' Valerie said tiredly. 'Do you honestly believe any human being could make three people vanish so completely?'

'It only looks like magic until you know how the trick is done,' I said.

'Do we have to keep going over this?' said Eileen. 'All these theories are making my head hurt.'

'My stomach hurts,' said Valerie.

Jimmy leaned in beside her, immediately concerned. 'Do you feel sick? Could it be something you ate?'

Valerie managed a small smile for him. 'Stop panicking, Jimmy. If it was the meal, we'd all be feeling it by now.'

'Just worried about you . . .' said Jimmy.

'It's only nerves,' said Valerie. 'My stomach aches because I'm tense all the time. Never able to relax, even for a moment, waiting for the next bad thing to happen. Waiting for someone else to disappear, and worrying that it might be me.'

'Like a solider in the trenches,' said Eileen. 'Listening for the next bullet and wondering whose name will be on it. Does it make me a bad person that I don't feel so bad about Albert being gone because I never really liked him that much? Not even back in the days when we were all supposed to be such good chums. I only put up with him because he was Olivia's boyfriend. He never bought a round and always depended on us for transport, and he let Olivia walk all over him.'

'He had his good points,' said Valerie.

'Name one . . .' said Jimmy.

'I thought he was your friend!' said Penny.

'He was,' said Jimmy. 'One of my oldest and closest friends. Doesn't mean I actually liked him all that much.'

'It's often that way,' said Eileen. 'Perhaps because we value our friends more and forgive them more. I will miss him.'

'You always knew where you were with Albert,' said Valerie. 'When the pressure was on and it really mattered, you could always rely on Albert to let you down.'

'And there's no denying he screwed us all royally over the Castle,' said Jimmy. 'Both Albert and Olivia did.'

'At least he'll never leave his precious inn now,' said Valerie.

'And you think that's a good thing?' said Jimmy.

'If we stay here much longer, we'll find out,' said Eileen.

'We're not staying,' I said. 'It's too dangerous. I know you're all reluctant to leave the inn because of the dark and what might be outside . . .'

'Yes!' said Jimmy. 'With good reason! At least in here we can see what's happening and defend ourselves!'

'And how has that worked out for you so far?' Penny said kindly. 'The light didn't protect Olivia, or Thomas or Albert. Ishmael is right. We have to get out of here while we still can. We know bad things happen here, we don't know that about the way back to town.'

'What if the hanging tree is back?' said Valerie.

'Then give it plenty of room,' I said. 'It might come and go, but it's still just a tree. I really don't think it's going to rip up its roots and chase us across the car park.'

'Oh thanks a whole bunch for that highly disturbing image!' said Jimmy. 'Like I needed something else to worry about.'

'But what if there is someone, or something, waiting for us out there?' said Valerie.

'Like the face at the window?' said Eileen.

'If there is a face I will punch it,' I said. 'And if there's a person attached, I will slam them up against the nearest wall until they start giving me answers as to what the hell is going on here.'

'Actually, I think I'd pay good money to see that . . .' said Jimmy.

'But what if we go outside,' Eileen said slowly, 'and there's nothing there?'

We all looked at her. Eileen's sour but determined strength seemed to have deserted her. She looked somehow smaller and less certain. Like a boxer in the ring who'd been hit too hard and too often. And there was something about her voice. She sounded . . . almost fey.

'What if the demon has opened a door big enough to swallow the whole inn?' she said. Her eyes were a little too large than was good for her, as she stared at something only she could see. 'What if we go outside and the world we know is gone, replaced by something else? What if there's nothing outside . . . and this is all there is now?'

For a long moment no one said anything.

'OK . . .' said Jimmy. 'Someone has just jumped right over the edge and taken common sense with her. You need a drink, Eileen.'

'Jimmy!' said Valerie. But her heart wasn't in it.

'Oh come on!' said Jimmy. 'The vicar's wife has lost the plot big time. This is crazy talk!'

'And what's happened already isn't insane?' said Valerie.

'No,' Penny said sharply. 'It's weird, but that doesn't make it crazy. Just something we don't understand yet.'

'Now we have to go outside,' I said. 'If only to reassure ourselves that the world is still out there.'

'Do we?' said Jimmy. 'Because if it has all gone away, I think I'd be much happier not knowing that.'

'We're going outside, Jimmy,' said Valerie. 'Because my stomach will never feel right again until I do.'

'The words "frying pan" and "fire" come to mind,' said Jimmy. 'And not at all in a good way.'

We all rose to our feet. Jimmy and Valerie had to help Eileen. Her mind had drifted off in a dangerous direction, and she couldn't seem to find her way back. Hopefully a good look around a perfectly ordinary car park would help put her back together again. Eileen had been the strongest member of the group; but the strongest are often the first to break, when they discover strength isn't enough to protect them or those they care about.

I organized everyone into a straight line, single file, with a hand on the shoulder of the person in front of them. I took the lead, and put Penny at the back again because I needed someone there I could trust. I marched them down the long room to the front door, and then stopped.

'You'd better put your coats on,' I said. 'It's cold outside. And once you've all seen that everything is as it should be, we are all of us walking back to town. No arguments, no detours, no hanging around.'

Nobody argued. Though they did look to me for permission
to take hands off shoulders before they went for their coats.
I nodded brusquely, and they rummaged quickly through the
pile of coats I'd dumped on the floor when I used the coat
stand to wedge the front door shut. I waited till they were all
done and back in line before I retrieved my coat. I shrugged
it on, and then couldn't resist checking my pockets. Just in
case my phone and car keys had magically reappeared. They
hadn't.

I went over to the front door, pulled the wooden coat stand
away and leaned it against the wall, and took hold of the door
handle. The door wouldn't open. I stepped back and stared
at it.

'Ishmael?' said Penny, from the back of the line. 'What's
the problem?'

'The door's locked,' I said.

'How is that even possible?' said Jimmy, so angry that for
a moment he actually forgot to be scared. 'We just used it,
only a few minutes ago!'

'How is any of this possible?' said Eileen. 'The inn has
gone bad. It's working against us.'

'Eileen, will you please go back to being a "quiet space"
case?' said Jimmy. 'I can cope with that better.'

'Screw you!' said Eileen.

Jimmy smiled suddenly. 'That's better. Much more you.'

Eileen managed a small smile for him.

'Someone is messing with us,' I said, 'they really don't
want us to leave. So they sneaked round and locked the door
from the outside. But that's not going to stop us. Penny, keep
a watch on the dining room while I sort this out in case it's
another distraction.'

'On it, darling,' said Penny.

'Is she always this positive?' said Jimmy.

'Mostly,' I said.

'How do you stand it?'

'Practice.'

I studied the closed door carefully. I couldn't open it with
a shoulder charge, like I had with the kitchen door, because
this one opened inwards.

'Would it be easier to smash one of the windows?' Jimmy said tentatively. 'Get out that way?'

'Given how thick those old-fashioned leaded glass windows are, I doubt it would be easy,' I said. 'And anyway, we'd be left with an opening we couldn't easily block off afterwards.'

'What does that matter?' said Valerie. 'We're not coming back. Are we?'

'We might have to,' said Eileen. 'If there's nowhere out there to go.'

'And I thought you were getting better . . .' said Jimmy.

'I do feel a bit better now we're doing something,' said Eileen. 'I'm just being practical.'

'You mean paranoid,' said Jimmy.

'Paranoid?' said Eileen. 'Is that what they're saying about me?'

And again, they shared a small smile. Valerie laughed quietly, just for a moment.

'We are leaving through the front door,' I said. 'I've got this.'

I reached into a hidden pocket in my coat and brought out a flat leather pouch. Unfolded, it contained a number of slim steel probes. Lock picks. I sorted through them carefully, looking for just the right tools to use on the old-fashioned lock.

'Wait a minute! Throw everything into reverse and slam on the brakes!' said Jimmy. 'Are those what I think they are? Where did you get them?'

'I do security work, remember?' I said. 'A lot of which can depend on my being able to get inside places where I'm not supposed to be.'

'Fair enough,' said Jimmy.

'Would they work on the cars?' Valerie asked hopefully.

'No,' I said. 'Now hush, children, and let me work.'

I had the lock open in a few moments, though I had to use a lot of strength to turn the heavy tumblers. One of the steel probes actually bent in half under the strain. I put the lock picks away, braced myself, and then opened the front door and pulled it all the way back. The car park was still there, completely deserted under the familiar star-speckled sky with its dull half moon. I looked back at the others.

'Everything outside is exactly as it should be. Dark and cold, and just a bit windy. Nothing at all to worry about. No hanging tree, no one peering in through the windows, and absolutely nothing between us and the road back to town. So get yourselves in line, people, hands back on shoulders. We are leaving, and we are not stopping for anything. Follow me.'

Outside in the car park the wind had died down but the air was freezing cold. Our breath steamed thickly. Moonlight shimmered across the open expanse, more than enough to let us see where we were going. Probably not enough to light the way once we were inside that long leafy tunnel through the woods, but the road was pretty straight, with no side turnings. I didn't see how we could get lost. As long as we stepped it out, we should be back at Black Rock Towen in no time.

'See?' I said, glancing back over my shoulder. 'Nothing's gone and nothing's changed. We're still exactly where we should be.'

'Sorry,' said Eileen. She was standing a little straighter now, as she looked out into the night, and her gaze was sharp and fierce again. 'I lost it there, for a while. But I'm back now.'

'Imagine my relief . . .' said Jimmy.

'Shut up, Jimmy!' said Eileen, and he nodded happily.

And then Eileen turned her head suddenly, to look back at the inn. We all turned to look, as well.

'What is it, Eileen?' said Valerie.

Eileen stared at the Castle. Bright light streamed from its windows and spilled out of the open door, but nothing was moving anywhere.

'Didn't you hear that?' she said.

We all looked at each other.

'Hear what?' said Jimmy.

'A voice, calling my name,' said Eileen.

'Oh hell!' said Jimmy. 'Are you hearing Voices now?'

'No!' said Eileen. 'It came from the Castle, not inside my head.'

'I didn't hear anything,' said Valerie, but her voice wasn't as certain as it might have been.

'Whose voice do you think it was, Eileen?' I said.

She shook her head slowly. 'I couldn't tell. But I think . . . it might have been Thomas, calling out to me. Afraid because I was going off and leaving him. I'm sorry, Ishmael, but I can't go with you. I can't leave Thomas here, on his own. The rest of you should still go, and send help once you've reached the town.'

She took her hand off Jimmy's shoulder and stepped out of the line. Then she took a deep breath and headed back to the front door.

'Oh hell!' said Jimmy. 'That's torn it.'

'We can't go off and leave her here,' said Valerie.

'No,' I said. 'We can't. You and Jimmy had better go after her. Penny and I will be along in a minute.'

Valerie and Jimmy hurried after Eileen.

'I didn't hear anything,' Penny said firmly. 'And I was right at the back of the line, closest to the open front door. Did you hear anything with your amazing augmented senses, space boy?'

'No,' I said. 'Of course, I was concentrating on where we were going. Damn it, Penny! We were so close to getting out of here.'

'Someone really doesn't want us to leave,' said Penny.

'I'll make them regret that,' I said.

'Of course you will,' said Penny.

We shared a quick smile, linked arms, and went after the others. Back to the inn, and what lay in wait for us.

When we stepped through the open door, Eileen was standing in the middle of the dining room, looking fiercely about her and listening hard. The room was empty, and there wasn't a sound to be heard anywhere. Jimmy and Valerie stood on either side of Eileen, being supportive. And to make sure she didn't go running off on her own. They were listening too, but it was obvious they weren't hearing anything. I closed the front door and jammed the coat stand back in place. More for the feeling of security it provided than because I had any faith in it.

'Hello?' Eileen said suddenly. 'Thomas, it's me! Eileen! I came back . . . Can you hear me?'

There was no reply. Eileen shook her head slowly, then turned to look back at me.

'It was just another distraction, wasn't it?'

'Probably,' I said.

'If someone is so determined to keep us from leaving, then we should go. If only to spite them,' said Eileen. 'But I can't. Not as long as there's a chance Thomas is still here and still needs me.'

'That's what the demon is counting on,' said Jimmy.

'But we can't leave Eileen!' Valerie said to him, pointedly.

'Of course not,' Jimmy said quickly. 'Old friends, together. One for all, and all of us screwed.'

'You had to go and spoil the moment, didn't you?' said Valerie.

'It's what I do best,' said Jimmy.

'I wish you were joking,' said Valerie.

And then she laughed and hugged Jimmy and Eileen, and they hugged her back. Old friends after all, that no one was going to separate.

'I suppose we'd better sit down at the table again,' I said, 'since we're clearly not going anywhere.'

'Don't be such a grouch,' said Valerie. 'Just because you weren't included in the hug.'

We sat down round the table again. I was getting pretty tired of looking at it. No one said anything for a while. So I decided I might as well get the ball rolling, if only by thinking out loud.

'If we can't escape the puzzle, we have to solve it. We have to figure out who is behind all of this, and what we can do to stop them.'

'You have to admire the man's blind optimism,' said Jimmy.

'They didn't have to stay,' said Valerie. She looked thoughtfully at me, and Penny. 'You could have walked back to Black Rock Towen and left us here to our fate. You're not scared of the dark, like we are.'

'I couldn't go off and leave you,' I said.

'Why not?' said Eileen.

'I feel responsible for you,' I said. 'How long do you think you'd last without me – and Penny, of course?'

'Nice save, sweetie,' said Penny. 'I only had to kick your ankle once.'

Jimmy was scowling. 'You didn't protect Olivia. Or Thomas or Albert.'

'They didn't listen to me,' I said.

'We can look after ourselves,' said Valerie. 'We're not children.'

'Except when we're afraid of the dark,' said Eileen.

'I'm still half convinced you two are part of the problem,' said Jimmy, switching his scowl from me to Penny and back again. 'Nothing out of the ordinary ever happened to any of us until you turned up.'

I started to say something, but stopped when Penny put a hand on my arm and squeezed it hard. She was quite right, of course. I'd already lost my temper in the kitchen, and it's never good for anyone when I lose control. I nodded to Penny.

'They may be annoying, but I still can't leave them.'

'Of course you can't,' said Penny. 'It's not in your nature. Even though they can be very annoying.'

'It's always possible someone was counting on that,' I said. 'That I wouldn't do the sensible thing and walk back to town.'

'Because, of course, it's always all about you,' said Jimmy.

'Actually, usually it is,' I said. 'But not this time . . . I think they were counting on you being a group of old friends who would never abandon each other. I think it's all about you. Only Penny was invited to join you at this special pre-opening meal, no one knew I was going to be here.'

Penny looked at me sharply. 'You think they were brought here on purpose? That they were targeted? Set up to be taken?'

'Don't you?' I said. 'Everything that's happened has the feel of something carefully worked out in advance. That's why the demon is taking people one at a time, to keep us off balance so we won't work out what's really going on. Someone wants to punish this group of old friends for past sins. You and I are merely collateral damage. In fact if we hadn't been here, everyone might have been taken by now.'

'So, we're back to it all being all about you . . .' said Jimmy.

'You don't believe there's anything unnatural going on here, do you, Ishmael?' said Penny.

'No,' I said.

'Stop talking about us like we're not here!' Jimmy said loudly.

'That *is* just a bit spooky, under the circumstances,' said Valerie.

'Just because we're not all holding hands for extra security and hanging on to your every word . . .' said Eileen.

I smiled around the table. 'I've been holding your hands for ages. That's why you're still here.'

'You're so full of it!' said Jimmy. 'In fact you are so full of it, it's a wonder it doesn't leak out of your ears when you cough.'

Penny laughed, but quickly smothered it when I looked at her.

'I'm missing something,' I said, with quiet dignity. 'Something about this place . . .'

'You always feel that way just before you work out what's really going on,' said Penny.

'I wish I had your confidence,' I said. 'This case is so different from what I'm used to. No bodies, no evidence, no clues . . . Nobody to interrogate and nothing to investigate. I feel lost.'

'I still don't like the way Albert just went off and left us,' said Penny, frowning fiercely. 'He must have known it was a dumb, even dangerous, thing to do . . . going into the kitchen on his own. But he didn't even hesitate. It almost seemed like he was in a hurry. Was he being influenced, do you think?'

'He didn't act like he was hearing Voices,' I said. 'And given how much we've discussed Voices this evening, I think he would have said something if he had been.'

'You're doing it again . . .' said Jimmy.

'Don't ignore us!' said Valerie. 'If you want to know anything about Albert, ask us. He was our friend.'

'Even if we didn't always like him that much,' said Eileen.

'And what did you mean when you said we were brought here to pay for our past sins?' said Valerie.

'Let's concentrate on Albert, for the moment,' I said. 'I'm still wondering what it was that he remembered so suddenly.

Something about which he didn't want to talk to us, and yet so important he was ready to go back into the room where his wife disappeared. Can any of you suggest what that might have been?'

'Perhaps he saw something in the kitchen earlier?' said Eileen. 'Something he didn't realize the significance of until now.'

'I tore that room apart,' I said, 'and couldn't find anything significant.'

'We did notice . . .' said Jimmy.

'Albert's behaviour didn't make any sense,' I said. 'But then not much about this case does.'

'I don't have any past sins I need to be punished for!' Valerie said loudly. 'None of us do.'

'At least nothing so bad that a demon would want to make us disappear because of them,' said Jimmy. 'Unless you've been holding back on us, Eileen.'

'I wish!' said Eileen. 'Vicar's wives don't have the time to get any serious sinning done.'

I looked around the dining room again, even though I knew I'd already seen everything there was to see. It didn't seem like a dangerous setting. Every detail was almost aggressively ordinary. But there was still a very real tension in the air. Because we all knew we couldn't trust anything about the room.

'I'd made myself accept that Thomas was dead,' said Eileen, 'that I'd never see him again . . . And then I heard him calling my name.'

'If it was Thomas . . .' said Jimmy.

'Someone called my name,' said Eileen. 'Called out to me for help. Who else would do that?'

'If someone's been lurking around listening to us . . .' said Jimmy.

'Or something,' said Valerie. She glared at me. 'Are you still not ready to admit there must be something supernatural after us?'

'There's no solid evidence . . .' I said.

'Exactly!' said Valerie. 'If this was just some crazy kidnapping stunt, there would be evidence. Clues as to what's going on. It's the complete lack of anything real and solid that proves this has to be a supernatural threat!'

There was a long pause.

'That really is pushing it a bit, Val,' said Eileen.

Jimmy grinned at her. 'You're back to your normal self.'

'I lapsed, for a while,' said Eileen. 'But everything's all right now.'

Then suddenly the lights went out. Darkness fell across the dining room, relieved only by the dim yellow glow of the single lit candle on the bar top. And then its light was snapped out, too. Complete and utter darkness filled the dining room from end to end, like a living thing. Even I couldn't see anything.

'Everyone stay where you are!' I said loudly. 'Reach out and grab each other's hands! Sing out when you've found someone!'

They all called out, one after the other. Penny's hand gripped mine tightly. I'd have known her touch anywhere.

'Stay where you are,' I said. 'Penny and I will light the candles.'

'It might be quicker if we all helped,' said Eileen.

'No it wouldn't,' I said. 'The last thing I need is all of you stumbling around in the dark, falling over each other and getting spooked.'

'Something is in the room with us!' said Valerie, her voice rising. 'Hiding in the dark!'

'No there isn't!' I said, just as loudly.

'How can you be sure?' said Jimmy.

'Because I'm not hearing anything moving about,' I said. 'Listen . . .'

And while they were busy doing that I rose to my feet and, taking Penny with me, went straight to the nearest candle. My memory worked perfectly well even in the dark. I found the box of matches by touch and lit the candle. Jimmy, Valerie and Eileen cried out in unison as the little light appeared, pushing back some of the darkness. I could just make them out, sitting close together at the table, and was quietly relieved they were all still there. I moved quickly round the dining room, lighting one candle after another, keeping Penny close at all times, until finally a long row of small bobbing lights filled the dining room with a pale yellow glow.

I'd been worried that Jimmy, Valerie or Eileen would silently disappear in the dark. That the blackout had been another distraction. But they were all still sitting round the table.

Suddenly Eileen pulled her hands free from the others and rose to her feet.

'That is it. That is the final straw that ruptured the camel's back. I want a drink. And I want it right now!'

'No you don't,' Valerie said immediately.

'Yes I bloody well do!' said Eileen. 'And the fact that I am perfectly ready to walk right over anyone who gets in my way is all the proof I need.'

She strode down the dining room to the bar and moved behind it to search for just the right drink. I didn't say anything, but I was disappointed in her. She'd been doing so well up till now. Jimmy and Valerie stood together at the table, unsure what to do.

'Please, Eileen, come back to the table,' said Valerie.

'When I'm ready,' said Eileen. 'When I've got a drink. You want me to bring you something?'

'Well . . .' said Jimmy.

'No you don't!' said Valerie.

'No I don't,' said Jimmy.

Eileen peered at the bottles stacked under the bar, and then knelt down and disappeared from sight. Jimmy and Valerie cried out involuntarily.

'Stop panicking!' said Eileen, from behind the bar.

'At least keep talking to us!' said Jimmy.

'Shut up, Jimmy,' said Eileen. 'I'm busy.'

Penny leaned in close to me. 'What was the point in cutting the power and plunging the whole place into darkness if the demon didn't intend to take advantage of it?'

'I don't know,' I said. 'To show us it's in control? To throw a scare into us . . . Hold it! Eileen, you've been quiet too long. You're scaring us! Please say something.'

But she didn't. I hurried down the dining room and looked behind the bar. There was no sign of Eileen anywhere. Jimmy and Valerie could tell what had happened from the look on my face. They made low moaning noises and held each other tightly.

'Poor Eileen!' Valerie said finally. 'I hope it isn't dark where she's gone. She was always so afraid of the dark, and what's in it.'

# SIX

## Death and the Demon

Jimmy and Valerie clung to each other like frightened children during a thunderstorm. Valerie didn't cry over Eileen's sudden disappearance, but Jimmy did. He just broke down suddenly, sobbing so hard his whole body shook. Valerie hugged him to her. The sound of Jimmy's weeping seemed to fill the whole room.

I looked everywhere behind the bar, but there was no sign of any struggle. Not even a scuff mark on the floor. I even knelt down to check the items stacked behind the bar, rummaged through the various bottles and usual boxes of snacks. Penny made an involuntary sound as I dropped down out of view and moved quickly forward so she wouldn't lose sight of me, even for a moment. I didn't know what I was looking for behind the bar. Whatever it was, I didn't find it.

I stood up and stamped hard on the floor, hoping for a hollow sound. All that happened was I hurt my foot. I grabbed hold of the wooden bar top with both hands, ready to tear the whole structure apart, but Penny made another sound. I made myself stop, and took my hands away. Smashing up the kitchen hadn't got me anywhere, and it had seriously freaked out the others. I didn't need Jimmy and Valerie even more upset than they already were. So I took a deep breath and stepped carefully back from the bar. I looked at Penny, and she moved quickly forward to be with me, comforting me with her presence.

'Are you all right?' I asked. My voice sounded harsh and strained, even to me.

'Not really,' said Penny. 'But I'm coping. Which is more than you can say for them.'

Jimmy had stopped crying, but he still looked like part of him had been torn away. Valerie was murmuring to him steadily. Low comforting sounds, like a mother with a child. I don't think Jimmy heard them, but perhaps it helped Valerie to have someone else to concentrate on. She turned her head suddenly, to glare at me.

'Why did Eileen disappear when she went behind the bar?' she said loudly. 'It was safe enough there before.'

'It wasn't the bar,' said Penny. 'It was the demon. Just waiting to carry Eileen off the moment she was out of our sight.'

'How could it know that?' said Valerie.

'Because it's watching us,' said Jimmy. His voice was flat, almost lifeless. 'It's been watching us all along.'

Valerie looked around her uncertainly. 'Could it be here in the room with us right now? Intangible and unseen, like in the old stories?'

I didn't say anything, because I had no answer for her. But I couldn't help feeling that, with my more than human senses, if anything unnatural was present in the room with us I would know. And I wasn't picking up anything.

'Is it too late to tie ourselves together with ropes?' said Jimmy, trying for a lighter tone and not even coming close.

'Albert said there aren't any ropes,' said Valerie.

'Then feel free to keep hold of me,' said Jimmy.

Valerie pushed him away from her, not unkindly. 'Looks like you're feeling better.'

'I'm not sure "better" is the right word,' said Jimmy. He scowled at the bar, and his mouth tightened into a flat line. 'I can't believe Eileen is gone.'

'She shouldn't have gone across to the bar on her own,' said Valerie.

'She needed a drink,' said Jimmy. His mouth twitched briefly. 'I always said it would be the death of her . . . But then she didn't have anything else.'

'She had her faith,' said Valerie. 'She was the one who brought Thomas into the Church in the first place. She knew it would be good for him. But her faith wasn't enough to protect her in this awful place. And the blessings we put down together weren't enough to save her, either. What could we have done to deserve this? What sins from our past could possibly justify what's been happening here?'

'If the demon was after us because of our sins, I would have been taken first,' said Jimmy.

Valerie managed a quick smile for him. 'You can't stand the thought of anyone being worse than you, can you?'

'A man has his pride,' said Jimmy.

'The demon only strikes when one of us is out of everyone else's sight,' I said. 'If each of us stays in plain sight of everyone else, it will have to step out into the light and reveal itself.'

'You say that as if you think that's a good thing!' said Jimmy.

'If I can see it, I can get my hands on it,' I said.

'You honestly believe you can fight a demon?' said Valerie.

'I have to believe that,' I said. 'That's what my whole life has been about.'

'Ishmael has fought some very dangerous things in his time,' said Penny. 'And he's still here, while they're not. That should tell you something.'

'What if it's already here but we can't see it?' said Jimmy. 'Because it's too much for our human minds to cope with. How can you fight something you're not capable of seeing or understanding . . .'

'This is no time to give up hope,' I said sternly.

'You will tell me when it is time, won't you?' said Jimmy. 'I'd hate to miss it.'

He was trying to be flippant, but his heart wasn't in it. He smiled briefly at Valerie.

'Maybe if you and I hold hands and refuse to let go, the demon will have to take both of us together. I don't think I'd feel so bad if we were to disappear at the same time. Wherever we end up, it might not be so bad if we're together.'

'All these years and you wait till now to learn how to be romantic!' said Valerie.

'Amazing what stress and sheer terror can bring out of you . . .' said Jimmy.

'Hold my hand and never let go,' said Valerie. 'And whatever happens, I will never let go of you.'

They clasped hands and stood together, smiling into each

other's eyes. Penny moved in close beside me, so we could talk quietly while they were busy immersed in each other.

'We can't stay here, Ishmael.'

'We only stayed because Eileen refused to leave,' I said. 'Now she's gone, I suppose there's nothing to keep us here.'

Jimmy's head snapped round. 'I heard that! Is that all Eileen's disappearance means to you? One less obstacle to doing what you want?'

'You can't honestly want to stay in this awful place,' said Penny.

'What if it was our trying to leave that made the demon take Eileen?' said Valerie. 'Nothing had happened for ages until we tried to escape.'

'You can't be serious!' I said.

'Try me!' said Valerie. 'We should never have listened to you.'

Jimmy smiled sourly at me. 'So that makes all of this your fault, Mister I'm the One in Charge.'

'We won't go,' Valerie said flatly. 'It's not safe out there. At least in here we've got a chance. Jimmy and I are staying put. You can't make us leave . . .'

'I don't think we'd be allowed to leave anyway,' said Jimmy. 'The demon would stop us, somehow.'

'We can't be sure of that,' I said.

'Yes we can!' said Valerie. 'Look around you, look at where the rest of us used to be!'

'We all need to sit down,' said Penny, carefully keeping her voice calm and reasonable, even though I could tell she was getting a bit tired of having to do that. 'It's been a long evening and we're all worn down.'

'We should never have come here,' said Jimmy. 'Like lambs to the slaughter.'

He led Valerie by the hand to the table, where they sat down heavily in their accustomed places. Penny and I joined them. And for a long moment we all just sat there, looking at each other.

'Do you think we'll die when the demon takes us?' Valerie said finally.

'I hope so,' said Jimmy. 'At least all this madness will be over then and I won't have to feel so scared all the time.'

'There's no evidence anyone is dead,' I said.

'Evidence?' said Valerie, her voice dangerously angry. 'You keep going on about proof and evidence! You really think things like that matter now?'

'They always matter,' I said. 'That's how we understand the world and what's happening in it.'

'I think we've moved way beyond that!' said Jimmy. 'This isn't the world I thought I knew.'

'There is a demon . . .' said Valerie. 'And it will come for us.'

'Then it had better kill me straight off,' I said. 'Because otherwise I will beat it to death with my bare hands. And if the others are still alive, even if they're in some other world, I will find a way to bring them home.'

'He means it,' Penny said brightly. 'Isn't he marvellous?'

'Men don't kill demons,' said Valerie.

'Then we'd better hope it's an alien,' I said.

'I could be dead before morning comes,' said Jimmy, almost wistfully. 'There's a thought I didn't expect to be having when I got out of bed this morning . . . Hell, I never thought I'd have to think about dying for years and years yet! I never even got around to making a will.'

'In my line of work you can't avoid thinking about it,' said Valerie. 'A lot of the old-time stories are really nothing more than extended metaphors for death and how to deal with it. I suppose it won't be so bad when we go, because we won't be leaving anyone behind.'

'That just makes it worse!' said Jimmy. 'No one left to give a damn that we're gone . . . As if our lives have made no mark on the world at all.'

'I'll care when you're dead,' said Valerie.

'And I will care about you,' said Jimmy. 'Though the way things are going, not for long.'

'I never thought my life would end like this,' I said. 'Sitting around helplessly, trapped by an unseen enemy for no reason I can understand.'

'I wonder what the Colonel will say when we're gone?' said Penny. She glanced at Jimmy and Valerie. 'Our boss.'

'Something irritated, no doubt,' I said. 'He'll miss us, right up to the point where he picks someone else to do our job.'

'For a long time after the rest of my family were killed,' said Penny, 'I didn't know how to feel. I kept wondering why I'd survived when everyone else had died. Why did I deserve to live? And then I realized. I lived because you saved me, Ishmael. So I decided I would justify my survival by working with you and saving others. I like to think I've made a difference. And we had fun, didn't we, Ishmael, defying the forces of darkness and doing things that mattered?'

'Yes,' I said. 'We did.'

Jimmy laughed harshly. There wasn't much humour in the sound. 'All those things I meant to do with my life! And I never did any of them because I was too busy doing other things.'

'You made a good living writing for the local paper,' said Valerie. 'Your work was always very . . . readable.'

'Oh, please!' said Jimmy. He didn't actually curl his lip, but he sounded like he wanted to. 'All I ever did was fill in the gaps between the adverts. Nothing I wrote ever mattered, never changed anything for the better. I did none of the things you're supposed to do when you're a journalist. When I'm gone and someone else takes over, the readers won't even notice. Except that the horoscopes will probably be a bit less depressing.'

'At least you got published,' said Valerie. 'All those books I meant to write, and I never even started one! I kept telling myself it was because I needed to do more research so I could produce the definitive account . . . But I was just putting off starting because I had no faith in my ability to do a decent job.'

'I had faith in you,' said Jimmy. 'I loved to hear you talk about the stuff you dug up. The old stories that everyone else had forgotten, and all your new insights into what they really meant. Out of all of us, I always believed you'd be the one to achieve something. To break out, get away, and be someone.'

'You should have told me,' said Valerie.

'I thought you knew,' said Jimmy.

They held hands tightly, clasped together on the table top.

They only had eyes for each other, so it was just as well Penny and I were keeping a watchful eye on our surroundings.

'What if we go to a better place?' Valerie said suddenly. We all looked at her, but she pressed on stubbornly. 'What if the demon takes us through its door, to its world . . . and it turns out to be a better world? We've all been assuming it's somewhere terrible, but . . . what if it's some kind of guardian angel and this is a rescue mission?'

There was a long pause as we all considered this new idea.

'If believing that makes you feel any better, you go right ahead,' Jimmy said finally.

'You don't?' said Valerie.

'It doesn't seem very likely, does it?' Jimmy said kindly.

'We should arm ourselves,' Penny said firmly. 'So we're in a position to fight back, whatever happens . . .'

'Arm ourselves?' said Jimmy. 'What with? Kitchen knives? Meat tenderizers? To take on something so powerful it can drag people away in complete silence, with not even a sign of a struggle?'

'That's your great idea, is it?' said Valerie. 'Make the demon angry? Aren't we in enough trouble as it is?'

'What else could it do to us?' said Penny.

'You really want to find out?' said Valerie.

'The best way to fight the demon is to make it impossible for it to take us,' I said. 'There's only four of us left now. Which makes it harder for the demon to trick us, or persuade us to go off on our own. We know better, now.'

'So did Eileen and Albert,' said Jimmy. 'And they still went.'

'We have to stick together,' said Penny. 'Be strong together.'

'I don't feel strong any more,' said Jimmy. 'Not that I ever did. I can't stand not knowing when my time will come. I just want it to be over, one way or another.'

'No you don't,' Valerie said firmly. 'That would be letting the demon win, and after everything that little shit has put us through I'm damned if I'll let it beat us. Man up, Jimmy! Our friends are gone. Be angry, like me.'

'I can't,' said Jimmy. 'There's not enough of me left.'

Valerie was holding Jimmy's hand firmly in both of hers and staring into his eyes. He was trying to care, for her sake.

Penny was scowling, thinking hard. I sat back in my chair and looked round the dining room yet again. Searching for something, any small thing I might have missed. The candle-lit room looked back at me, calm and quiet and subtly menacing. Like it knew something I didn't.

'Be honest with us, Ishmael,' said Jimmy. 'You and Penny have encountered weird shit before, haven't you? I can tell, because you're not freaking out like the rest of us. Have you ever come across anything like this?'

'No,' I said. 'Not like this. It's a mystery. But I will find the answer to what's going on. It's what I do.'

'It is. It really is,' said Penny. 'And he's very good at it.'

'I think Olivia and Albert and Thomas and Eileen might choose to disagree,' said Jimmy, 'if they were still here.'

'If the old stories teach us anything,' Valerie said slowly, 'it's that some mysteries have no answer. That's why the stories get passed down from generation to generation. Because the truth contained in them is just too big for us.'

'I've never believed that,' I said, a little more forcefully than I intended. 'Every mystery has an answer, every puzzle a solution. If we just dig deep enough and don't give up.'

'I'd like to give up,' said Jimmy. 'I can't help thinking it would feel really good to throw in the towel and stop struggling. To be able to relax at last, and not have to worry about anything.'

'You'll do no such thing!' Valerie said immediately. 'Because if you stop fighting, I'm lost as well.'

Jimmy smiled at her ruefully. 'You always did fight dirty, Val. You know I'd rather die than let you down.'

'Yes,' said Valerie. 'I've always known that.'

'Why did we break up?' said Jimmy.

'Because you're impossible to live with,' said Valerie.

'Really?' said Jimmy. 'I thought that was you.'

Valerie leaned forward, so their heads were close together. 'If we do somehow survive this, I am never letting go of you again.'

'You had to say "if", didn't you?' said Jimmy.

They laughed quietly together. Jimmy looked at me.

'How long have you and Penny been an item?'

'Just under four years,' Penny said briskly. 'It's never any good asking Ishmael about things like that, he's never been any good about dates. He'd forget our anniversary if I let him. Ishmael isn't the easiest person to live with either, but I can't imagine life without him.'

'You may have to,' said Jimmy. 'If he disappears before you do.'

'If he does, I'll go after him and bring him back,' said Penny.

'She would, too,' I said.

'Good luck with that!' said Jimmy.

'Jimmy!' said Valerie.

'People have been saying my name in exactly that tone of voice for years,' said Jimmy. 'And I've never understood why.'

'You're the only one who doesn't,' said Valerie. And then she stopped, as a thought struck her. 'Albert and Olivia are gone, Thomas and Eileen are gone. That's two couples. And now there are two couples left.'

Jimmy looked at her sharply. 'You think that means something?'

'It has to mean something,' said Valerie. 'Everything has to mean something. It's the only hope we've got.'

'The others weren't taken as couples,' I said. 'They went separately. Not even one after the other.'

'All right,' said Jimmy. 'It's my turn to have an idea. If the demon wants couples, why don't you and Penny volunteer to be taken? If you went willingly, that might please the demon so much it would let Val and me go.'

'Jimmy!' said Valerie. She sounded honestly outraged, but I couldn't help noticing the speculative look she turned on me and Penny.

'You really think that would work?' I said.

'I'd sacrifice the two of you to save Valerie,' said Jimmy.

'I wouldn't want that,' said Valerie.

'I'd do it anyway,' said Jimmy. 'Because I'd rather have you around to be mad at me than not have you at all. Because you matter to me, and they don't.'

'That's actually rather sweet, in a heartless sort of way,' said Valerie.

'I thought so,' said Jimmy.

'Don't we get a say in this?' said Penny.

'Of course!' Jimmy said earnestly. 'That's the whole point. A willing sacrifice. Like throwing a virgin into the volcano to appease the gods . . . Ishmael keeps saying he'll do anything to protect us. This is his chance to prove it.'

'You're grasping at straws,' I said. 'Still . . . our unseen enemy does like to make a point of staying unseen while he works. Maybe volunteering to be taken together, while remaining in the light, would be enough to tempt the demon out of hiding.'

Penny stared at me. 'You're not seriously considering this, are you?'

'I'm asking you to do this because it's the right thing to do,' I said. 'And because I'm damned if I can think of anything else.'

'Oh hell!' said Penny. 'If you put it like that . . . Go for it, space boy!'

'On it, spy girl,' I said.

'I hate cutesy nicknames,' said Jimmy.

I walked into the middle of the room, and Penny came with me.

'I need to fight back,' I said quietly.

'I know,' said Penny. 'I'm in the mood to kick the crap out of something.'

'Never knew you when you weren't,' I said generously.

'You say the sweetest things, darling,' said Penny. 'Shall we make a start in the kitchen? It's the only location from which two people have vanished.'

I moved over to the closed kitchen door and kicked it all the way open. The kitchen was full of shadows, but candlelight spilled in from the dining room. The floor was covered with wreckage, and some of the fittings hung drunkenly away from the walls. The whole place looked like a raging storm had hit it, and in a way it had. Penny squeezed into the doorway beside me. As much for company as to show solidarity. I heard Valerie push her chair back, get to her feet, and head in our direction.

'Val! No!' Jimmy yelled at her loudly.

'I need to know what's happening,' said Valerie. But her footsteps stopped a cautious distance short of Penny and me.

I heard Jimmy push back his chair. 'Stay where you are, Val. I'm coming to join you. I don't want us to be separated, even for a minute.'

'Don't start getting clingy, Jimmy,' said Valerie. 'I'm beginning to remember why we split up. I can look after myself.'

'Just wait for me,' said Jimmy. 'And then you can look after both of us.'

'Stay together,' I said loudly, not looking back from the kitchen. 'Penny and I are the bait. That's the point.'

'And if it should all kick off,' said Penny, 'Ishmael is going to need room to work. You don't want to get demon blood on you, do you?'

'I could live with that,' said Jimmy.

I stepped carefully forward into the kitchen, gesturing for Penny to stay in the doorway. I heard Jimmy and Valerie moving forward, despite everything I'd said, and when I glanced back they were peering fascinated over Penny's shoulders. They had the grace to look a little embarrassed. I turned my attention back to the kitchen.

'Well?' Penny asked impatiently. 'What do you see?'

'Something about the mess on the floor looks different,' I said.

Penny took a step forward, into the kitchen. Jimmy and Valerie didn't.

'How can you tell, Ishmael? When you decide to wreck a place, you don't hold back.'

'Something walked through this mess,' I said. 'Someone has been in the kitchen since we left.'

Penny moved quickly forward to stand beside me. 'Wouldn't we have heard a demon walking about in here?'

'How much noise does a demon make when it goes walking in the world?' I said.

'Or an alien?'

'Precisely. But it does make a mark. Some of this mess has been moved.'

'Jimmy, you stay right where you are!' Valerie said loudly,

behind us. 'I'm not going in there to join them and neither should you.'

'I'm just taking a quick look,' said Jimmy, contrary as always. 'Come with me and see for yourself.'

'I don't want to see,' said Valerie. 'I don't think I even want to know. Is there a trail of slime on the floor, Ishmael? Or maybe the smell of brimstone?'

'No and no,' I said. 'You really are a traditionalist, aren't you . . .? Jimmy, why are you standing behind me peering over my shoulder?'

'It really is gloomy in here,' said Jimmy. 'How do you see anything?'

'Training,' I said, 'and lots of carrots. There's a definite trail, from just inside the door to the right-hand wall.'

'I'm sorry, Ishmael,' said Penny. 'But I'm not seeing it.'

'Maybe you're just seeing what you want to see,' said Jimmy.

'The path is there,' I said.

'Come and take a look at this, Val,' said Jimmy. 'See if you can spot what he's talking about.'

'Val?'

Something in his voice made me turn round. The kitchen doorway was empty. I pushed past a shocked and trembling Jimmy and looked through the doorway into the dining room. There was no sign of Valerie anywhere. She'd been taken, softly and silently, while we weren't looking. Penny came forward and grabbed hold of my arm with both hands. Jimmy made a low, lost sound and ran through the doorway, back to our table, as though he half expected to find Valerie still sitting there, waiting for him. He looked wildly about him, and then threw the table over on its side. He stared down at the bare floor, breathing hard.

'It should have been me!' he said. 'I was ready to go . . . The demon must have heard me, so why did it take her? She had so much to live for, and I don't. She had a future, but I don't. Why did it take her?'

'Because she was on her own,' I said. 'And none of us were looking.'

Jimmy glared around the room with wild eyes. 'Give her

back!' he screamed at the walls. 'You can have me, if you'll just give Valerie back!'

There was no response. Jimmy suddenly collapsed, sat down hard on the floor like a toddler who's lost all the strength in his legs. He hugged himself tightly, rocking back and forth.

'What's the point?' he said. 'What's the point of anything . . .? I was ready to go with her. I wouldn't have put up a fight, I would have just gone . . . Why didn't the demon take you and Penny?' He looked at me sullenly. 'It was supposed to take you and leave Val and me alone. That was the plan.'

'It seems the demon isn't interested in volunteers,' I said.

Jimmy surged up on to his feet again. 'This is all your fault! Bastard! If you hadn't lured me into the kitchen, I'd never have let go of Valerie's hand. Never taken my eyes off her to look for your damned evidence. If you hadn't made me turn my back on Valerie, she'd still be here.'

He ran straight at me and lashed out with his fist, catching me by surprise. But I was still able to pull back my head so he only caught me a glancing blow on the nose. Jimmy drew back his fist for another blow . . . and then stopped, his arm dropping limply to his side. He looked at me with wide, horrified eyes.

'You . . .!' he said. 'It's you!'

'What are you talking about?' I said.

'Ishmael,' said Penny. 'Your nose . . .'

I put my fingertips to my nostrils, and when I brought them away they were wet with blood. My golden blood. The last trace of my alien heritage.

'Demon!' said Jimmy, his voice was full of betrayal. 'It was you all along! Watching and listening, pretending to be one of us so you could prey on us unsuspected . . . You took my friends!'

'Jimmy, no . . .' I said.

I moved towards him, and he turned and ran. He got to the front door, hauled the coat stand out of the way, pulled the door open, and ran out into the night. I was already racing after him, with Penny close behind, but the door swung shut before I could get to it. I grabbed hold of the door handle, half expecting the door to be locked again and ready to rip the whole thing off its hinges if need be, but it opened easily.

I stepped outside and looked around. The car park was empty. No sign of Jimmy anywhere, and nowhere he could have gone.

Penny moved in beside me and put a comforting hand on my arm. 'He didn't understand.'

'He ran from me,' I said. 'When all I wanted to do was protect him. He ran from me, straight into the demon's arms.'

'It must have been waiting out here,' said Penny. 'But how could it have known . . .'

'Why didn't it come after us in the kitchen?' I said.

'Because it knew a trap when it saw one,' said Penny. 'At least Jimmy is with Valerie now.'

'You think that's a good thing?'

'Let's hope so.' Penny put her hand in mine. 'Hold on to me, Ishmael. Never let me go.'

'Never,' I said.

We went back into the Castle, and I closed the door on the night.

# SEVEN

## If These Walls Could Speak

Penny and I stood back to back in the middle of the dining room. I could feel her shoulder blades pressing up against mine, so we could be sure of each other's presence as we watched the room between us. It was all very quiet and very still. The candle flames burned steadily, untroubled by even a breath of air. Their yellow glow filled the long room from one end to the other and there was nothing, nothing at all, to see.

'No one else is in here with us,' I said. 'I'd know. I'm sure I'd know.'

'Why are we still here?' said Penny. 'We should leave, right now. Just run to the door and not stop running till we hit the town.'

'That would be the logical thing to do,' I said. 'But I'm too angry to be logical. I promised I'd protect the others but they were still taken, one by one. There have been cases where I couldn't save everyone, but this is the first time I couldn't save anyone.'

'You've still got me,' said Penny.

'I know,' I said. 'And I don't want to risk losing you too. You can go, if you want. I'll do something to hold the inn's attention.'

'Leave you here on your own?' said Penny. She grabbed me by the arm and spun me round forcibly, so she could glare into my face. 'You wouldn't last five minutes without me, and you know it. Besides, I can be just as heroic and insufferably self-righteous as you, if I put my mind to it.'

'I've always thought so,' I said. 'But, Penny, I can't leave here until I find out what's happened to all the missing people. I just can't. I have to try to save some of them. Or if that turns out not to be possible, at least avenge them.'

'Of course you do, sweetie,' said Penny. 'So, what's the plan? Tell me you have a plan.'

'You'd think I would have one by now, wouldn't you?' I said. 'But even after everything that's happened I still haven't got a clue as to what it is we're dealing with. I don't know whether it's a demon or an alien. Or something else entirely.'

'I think it all comes down to the inn,' said Penny. 'Nothing started happening here until the Calverts began their renovations and made major changes to the physical structure of the place. Maybe that altered something . . . or woke something up. What if we just tear the whole place apart and undo all the changes? Maybe that will put everything back to normal again.'

'The structure . . .' I said. And just like that, I got it. The one clue I needed, and everything fell into place. 'That's it, Penny! The missing people have to be somewhere. If they aren't inside the inn and aren't outside, where does that leave? Remember what Albert said about rats in the walls!'

'Slow down, Ishmael!' said Penny. 'I don't understand. What have the rats got to do with anything?'

'Not the rats,' I said. 'The walls. What's the one thing we always search for when impossible things start happening in an old building? Hidden doors and secret passageways. Concealed ways for people to come and go and move around unseen.'

'But the Calverts told us there weren't any,' said Penny. 'The builders didn't uncover anything like that . . .'

'And I think I know why,' I said. 'Look at the outer walls, Penny. Look at the thickness of the walls! Albert and Olivia told us they were at least two feet thick, but when I checked the upstairs windows earlier I could see how deeply inset they were. I'd say these walls are more like three feet thick. And why would an inn need walls that solid?'

'To protect the smugglers from attack?' said Penny.

'All the Revenue Men would have to do is surround the inn and starve them out,' I said. 'The smugglers would be trapped in here. No, these walls were very carefully constructed, for another purpose entirely.'

I moved over to the outer wall on the other side of the bar and studied the old stone carefully. Then I punched the wall, putting all my strength into the blow. I hit the wall again and again, alternating my fists, getting a rhythm going. The old stone pulverized and flew apart under the relentless pounding, and jagged cracks opened up in the wall. Because the wall before me wasn't nearly as thick as it appeared.

Golden blood flew from my knuckles, but I didn't stop. I grimaced fiercely as the old stone shattered under my fists. It felt good to be taking out my frustrations on something solid. Pain jarred through my hands and up my arms, but I wouldn't even let myself slow down until I'd opened up a big enough gap. Nothing was going to stop me now I was getting close to the truth at last. Close to all the answers to everything that was going on in the Castle. I finally stopped and stepped back, and just stood there for a moment breathing hard. The opening I'd made was more than big enough to reveal the tunnel hidden inside the wall, stretching from one end of the inn to the other. I took a deep breath to settle myself, and then nodded to Penny.

'There has to be a hidden door here somewhere, but I needed to do that.'

'Oh Ishmael,' Penny said quietly. 'What have you done to your hands?'

'It was worth it,' I said. Though the smile I showed her probably wasn't very reassuring. I glanced down at the golden blood dripping from my clenched fists.

The tunnel consisted of two very thin walls forming a long narrow passageway, lit by a series of candles carefully set in niches at intervals along it. While I examined the tunnel, Penny found some napkins behind the bar and insisted on wrapping them round my damaged hands. I let her do it. I was still thinking hard, putting all the clues together. Penny finally finished and moved in beside me, and peered disgustedly down the hidden tunnel.

'We should have known,' she said. 'No demon did this. And no alien, either. The inn must have been built this way by the original smugglers. All the exterior walls must be hollow!'

'And all those old stories, about ghosts and monsters and general weird shit, were nothing more than simple misdirection,'

I said. 'Designed to keep us from realizing it was just people behind the disappearances.'

'But who could it be?' said Penny. 'We're the only ones left! Everyone else has been taken. Could someone else have been hiding in these walls all along, unknown to everyone, all through the evening?'

'No,' I said. 'This could only have been planned by someone who knew the structure of the Castle inside and out. It has to be Olivia and Albert. They must have discovered evidence of the tunnels' existence during the renovations and kept it to themselves. The builders were concentrating on the interior, so it wouldn't have been difficult. And having found the tunnels, it would only have been a matter of time and persistence for Albert and Olivia to search out all the hidden entrances in the walls. Which provided them with all the ways they needed to appear and disappear at will.

'Olivia disappeared first, using a hidden door in the kitchen. One of its walls is an outer wall, just like this one. That set up the idea of someone vanishing from a room without any explanation. After that she just moved back and forth through the tunnels, from wall to wall, listening to us.'

'And Albert was in on it the whole time?' said Penny.

'He had to be,' I said.

'But he seemed so upset after his wife disappeared!'

'Acting,' I said. 'Remember, Albert told us that one of his occupations in London was running murder mysteries. So he was used to improvising and thinking on his feet, under pressure, to keep the story going. His reactions to the situation helped keep us scared and confused. And he could always sink into his shocked daze when he didn't want to answer questions.'

'He did seem to snap in and out of that a bit too easily,' said Penny.

'Olivia overheard everything from inside the tunnels,' I said. 'And produced whatever off-stage noises or actions were needed to maintain an atmosphere of panic and terror that would keep everyone from thinking too clearly. And when we sensibly decided to leave the inn, Albert was the one who announced that he had seen the hanging tree out in the car park and frightened people so much they refused to go. Then, when he finally thought he might be starting to look a little suspicious, he suddenly remembered something important in the kitchen and disappeared through the same hidden door his wife had used.'

'It was Olivia's face at the window!' said Penny.

'Probably wearing a cheap fright mask,' I said. 'No doubt there are exterior doors in the walls as well, which allowed them to move around outside. Olivia was able to lock the front door because she had all the keys to the Castle.'

'All right,' said Penny. 'Since you're on a roll, what happened to everyone's car keys and phones?'

'I've been thinking about that,' I said. 'Once I knew it had to be Albert and Olivia, the answer was obvious. They were our hosts for the evening, so what could be more natural than for them to take our coats as we arrived and hang them on the coat stand? Which provided plenty of time for one of them to search through the pockets and take what they needed, while the other kept the coats' owners distracted with hospitable talk. And they must have picked a few trouser pockets as well, where necessary. Which makes me wonder what else they got up to in London that they didn't like to talk about.'

'What about the landline?' said Penny. 'Did Olivia cut the wires?'

'Probably simpler than that. Albert just said the phone was dead, and we believed him. He did it so convincingly none of us ever thought to check for ourselves.'

'Did Olivia put out the lights?'

'Of course,' I said. 'She knew where the fuses are. And it was Olivia who produced all the spooky noises during the seance, from inside the walls. Helped along by some cueing from Albert, no doubt.'

'OK,' said Penny. 'I'll bite. But why are the walls so hollow?'

'Think of the inn's name,' I said. 'The Castle. Everyone thought the walls were built especially strong and thick in order to keep enemies out. But castles are places you fight back from, which is not the smugglers' way. They were thieves, not fighters, more used to disappearing when threatened. So the smugglers designed and built an inn with hollow walls that they could disappear into when necessary and not be found. I'll bet you good money the tunnels connect to a hidden way down through the cliff to the beach below. So smuggled goods could be transported up to the inn in secret.'

'All those old stories about people who went missing inside the Castle,' said Penny, 'were started by the smugglers to scare people off!'

'And possibly to explain the sudden disappearance of people who knew too much about the smugglers' business,' I said.

Penny peered down the long tunnel again. 'Do you think the missing people are in the walls somewhere?'

'No,' I said. 'That's where they must have been taken at first, but they would then have been moved somewhere else. To a cellar, perhaps.'

'Which is why people only disappeared when no one was watching,' said Penny. 'Because otherwise we would have seen it was Olivia or Albert. They just stepped out of a hidden door, grabbed their victims, and dragged them into the nearest hollow wall . . . But why did none of their victims put up a fight? Thomas was bigger and stronger than both the Calverts put together. And what was the point of all this, anyway?'

'I say we go into this tunnel and find out where it leads,' I said. 'Then find the Calverts and ask them.'

Penny looked at me sharply. 'What if they've been listening to us all this time?'

'They don't appear to be in this wall,' I said. 'Hopefully they're somewhere else, dealing with their last few victims.'

Penny gave me a steady look. 'Do you think any of the missing people could still be alive?'

'It seems unlikely,' I said. 'But I have to believe there's still a chance to save someone.'

'Of course you do,' said Penny. 'How are your hands?'

I looked down at my bandaged hands. Golden stains showed on the napkins.

'The bleeding's stopped,' I said. 'You know I heal quickly.'

'Not that quickly,' said Penny.

'All right,' I said. 'If there's any fighting to be done, you can do it.'

'You're too kind,' said Penny.

'I've always thought so,' I said.

I led the way into the tunnel. The hollow between the two thin walls was so narrow I had to turn almost sideways to move along it. And every now and again I had to get down and crawl on all fours to scramble underneath the inset windows. The candles burned brightly in the walls, lighting the way.

'This is why Albert had so many candles in stock!' I said.

'I'm still trying to figure out how they took Thomas from inside the toilet,' said Penny.

'The toilet must have backed on to an outer wall,' I said, 'with a hidden door that opened directly into the room. Thomas never even saw them coming. No wonder he never got a chance to fight back.'

'They got him while he was sitting on the throne?' said Penny. She shuddered briefly. 'That's creepy!'

'All of this is,' I said.

At the end of the wall a set of rough stone steps led steeply down. I followed them all the way down until they ended at a simple wooden door. I stopped before it, pressed my ear against the wood, and listened carefully. Penny waited behind me, trusting to my more than human senses to warn of any danger. I didn't hear anything, so I straightened up and tried the handle. The door wasn't locked. But then, why would it be? The Calverts thought they were the only ones who knew about it.

On the other side of the door was a great stone chamber, a massive open space almost the size of the inn above. Old-fashioned oil lamps and storm lanterns glowed on all sides, illuminating the Castle's cellar – the fabled lost store-room of the smugglers.

The missing guests – Thomas and Eileen, Jimmy and Valerie – hung lifelessly side by side from an old iron clothes rack. Heavy steel butcher's hooks had been forced through their shoulders, so that they hung like fresh deliveries in a meat locker. Their faces were empty of all expression, their eyes staring at nothing, but I still felt like they were looking at me accusingly, accusing me for having failed to save them. Penny made a soft shocked sound deep in her throat, and put a hand to her mouth. I started to say something, but she shook her head fiercely. She was already back in control. Neither of us were strangers to bodies, or sudden death, any more.

I moved in closer. There were no obvious wounds or causes of death, and hardly any blood around the hooks in their shoulders, suggesting they'd been dead before they were hung up. A strange smell touched my nostrils, becoming clearer as I leaned in to study their faces. A rich, cloying smell. Like rotting flowers.

'You couldn't have saved any of them, Ishmael,' said Penny. 'You never had a chance.'

'I know,' I said. 'But that doesn't help. It still feels like I let them down.'

Penny started to put a hand on my arm, and then stopped. When she spoke again, her voice was all business.

'How did they die?'

'No obvious signs,' I said, stepping back. 'Just this odd smell . . .'

'I don't see Albert and Olivia here anywhere.'

'We can be sure now that they weren't among the victims,' I said. 'Or they'd be hanging with the others. They must be the killers, and they must be around here somewhere.'

'Want to check the walls?' said Penny.

'These walls would have to be solid,' I said. 'To support the weight of the inn above.'

It didn't take long to search the cellar. There was no trace of the smugglers' fabled lost treasure, just a few old wooden crates and some dusty bottles. The stone floor and walls were the same dirty grey; and heavily flecked with mould, suggesting no one had been down here in some time.

'Do you think there was ever anything valuable down here?' said Penny.

'I doubt it,' I said. 'Smugglers dealt in food and wine and other taxable items, not gold or silver or jewels.'

Another door at the far end of the cellar opened on to another series of stone steps, dropping away further than even my sight could follow. All the way down through the cliff to the beach, probably. More lit candles, in niches in the walls, showed that someone had used the stairway recently.

'The Calverts must be checking their escape route,' I said.

'Do we go after them?' said Penny.

'No need,' I said. 'I can hear footsteps. They're coming back up.'

I carefully closed the door, backed away, and took another quick look around. 'Albert and Olivia must have discovered all of this during the renovations and taken pains to keep it secret from the builders. I wonder how long it took them to work out how you make people disappear in plain sight.'

'But why?' said Penny. 'Why did they want to kill their oldest friends? And why invite me here?'

'We did it for revenge,' said Olivia.

I looked round unhurriedly as Albert and Olivia emerged from the doorway. Penny stuck close beside me, almost quivering with suppressed anger. The Calverts didn't seem surprised to see us; or guilty, or even scared. Just annoyed at being caught out. Olivia looked at Penny and me as though we were nothing more than an inconvenient interruption in her marvellous plans. Albert just looked sullen.

'You shouldn't be here,' he said. 'This is our place.'

'Hush, dear,' said Olivia. 'I'll do the talking.' She smiled at me, ignoring Penny. 'You've worked it all out, haven't you?'

'Most of it,' I said.

'I always knew you were the clever one,' said Olivia. 'I knew you'd be trouble, the moment I met you.'

'Why did you kill your friends?' Penny asked harshly.

'Let me tell them, Olivia,' said Albert. 'I want them to know how stupid they've been.'

'Tell them, Albert,' said Olivia.

'It was easy,' he said, beaming with pride. 'When Olivia and I researched the tansy pudding to make sure we were using a safe dosage, we discovered a long forgotten text that described the poison Tyrone put in his final meal. It was derived from the tansy flowers. The text also showed how the poison could be reduced to a powder which, when breathed in, would render the victim sedated and tractable, before it killed them.

Tyrone never used it that way, as far as we know, but it seemed a simple enough process.'

'So all I had to do,' said Olivia, 'was appear suddenly from nowhere, catching my victims by surprise, and blow a handful of the powder into their mouth and nose.'

'Of course,' I said. 'I smelt it on their faces.'

'They saw me as a fellow victim, not a threat,' Olivia said happily. 'Which bought me all the time I needed. They never even got a chance to make a sound. Then all I had to do was take them through the nearest door into the wall. There are hidden entrances all over the place, designed by the smugglers to open and close silently. All it took was a lot of practice and a steady nerve.'

She stepped forward, stuck out an open palm heavy with dust, and blew it into my face. Too late, Penny cried out a warning. Smiling at Olivia and Albert, I stood there and breathed the stuff in.

'Sorry to disappoint you,' I said, 'but I'm immune to most poisons.'

'So that's why the drink didn't affect you!' said Olivia.

'What drink?' said Penny, moving in close beside me to make sure I was OK.

'We put tansy poison in the plum brandy, so we could get him out of the way,' said Albert. 'Just one glass should have been enough to make him appear drunk and helpless. But instead, he drank the whole bottle and it didn't even touch him!'

'How is that possible?' asked Olivia, glaring at me. 'How could you be immune to a poison that no one's even heard of in centuries?'

'His hands!' Albert said suddenly. 'Olivia! Look at his hands!'

I looked down at my bandaged hands and then held them up so the Calverts could see the golden bloodstains clearly. For the first time, the studied arrogance slipped from their faces. Presented with something beyond their experience, all their marvellous plans and underhand methods went for nothing. For the first time, they looked scared. As they looked at my hands.

'What are you?' said Olivia.

'Very angry,' I said. 'Tell me about the concealed entrances.'

'They were put in place while the inn was being built,' said Olivia, still staring numbly at my hands. 'Because we told you there weren't any hidden doors or secret passageways, and I was the first to disappear, it never occurred to you to disbelieve us and check for yourself. If you'd taken the time to look closely, you would have seen them. But we kept you too busy thinking about other things . . .'

'You were our hosts,' said Penny. 'We trusted you.'

'You should have known better,' said Olivia. 'Nothing good ever came out of the Castle.'

'Why?' I said. 'Why did you do all this? Why go to so much trouble to kill your oldest friends?'

'They were never our friends,' said Albert. 'Not really. They drove us out of Black Rock Towen when the original deal for the Castle fell through and they lost all their precious savings. They blamed us, even though none of it was our fault.'

Olivia glared at Penny. 'We did our best to make the deal work. And it would have, if not for your father!'

'He promised us we could have the money we needed,' said Albert. 'And we all committed ourselves to the deal on the strength of his promise and his business reputation.'

'And then he let us down,' said Olivia. 'And our so-called friends decided it was all our fault. They spread word around the town that we were not to be trusted. No one would even talk to us. We had to go away to London to start again. But we always said we'd be back some day, to have our revenge.

'Finally, after all these years, the lottery win made that possible. We bought the inn and started the renovations, originally with perfectly straightforward intentions. We were going to turn the Castle into a successful business and then rub our friends' noses in it, prove to them that we could do what they couldn't. But then the idea came to us of a far more personal and satisfying revenge. That's why we invited our old friends here this evening for this very special meal. And that's why we invited you, Penny. We'd much rather have taken our revenge on your father; but since he was dead, we settled for you. The sins of the father and all that . . .'

'We weren't expecting you to bring someone with you,' said Albert. 'And certainly not someone so troublesome.'

'You nearly spoiled everything,' said Olivia.

'You planned this whole evening just to kill your friends?' said Penny.

'Not just kill them,' said Olivia. 'Death on its own wasn't enough to balance the books. Not after everything they'd put us through. All those years in London slaving over jobs we knew weren't worthy of us. It was only fitting that our friends' deaths should be part of restoring our fortunes to what they should have been. They, and you, were going to just disappear. Vanish into thin air, with not a trace remaining to explain what had happened and only Albert and I left to tell the tale . . . And what a tale it would have been! A party of old friends who gathered together to celebrate Tyrone's infamous meal and were never seen again. The publicity would have been incredible. There's nothing like an unsolved mystery to bring the customers pouring in.'

'We had the whole story worked out long before any of you arrived,' said Albert, smirking proudly. 'Our very own murder mystery. All you had to do was disappear, with a little help from us.'

'But why stretch it out, taking one person at a time?' I said. 'Why not just poison the meal like Tyrone did, and dispose of our bodies afterwards?'

'Where would the fun have been in that?' said Olivia. 'All of you had to suffer. Just as we were made to suffer.'

'And to keep you from working out what was happening,' said Albert, 'I was right there with you all along. Playing with you, messing with your minds, and loving every moment of it.'

'He was very convincing, wasn't he?' said Olivia. 'I always said he should have been on television.'

'You got a taste for that while you were running your murder mysteries in London, didn't you?' I said.

'Got it in one,' said Olivia. 'Albert provided the cues, and I responded. Especially during the seance. We had you all shaking in your boots.'

Penny gestured angrily at the four bodies hanging from the iron rack. 'This wasn't a game! Your friends are dead!'

'They had it coming,' said Albert. 'All of them.'

'And me?' said Penny. 'You were always so kind to me when I was a child.'

'If you can't hurt the one you hate,' said Olivia, 'hurt the one you can reach.'

'The game is over now,' I said. 'You lose.'

'Not necessarily,' said Olivia. 'I wonder . . . The tansy dust didn't affect you, but what about Penny?'

'Yes!' said Albert. 'Do it, Olivia!'

'Why not?' said Olivia. 'You messed up my lovely plan, Ishmael. Someone has to suffer for that.'

'We put all our money into the Castle,' said Albert. 'Everything we had. This plan has to succeed, or we'll be ruined. And maybe a strong enough dose will do you in too, Ishmael. Whatever you are.'

'I won't be cheated out of my fortune again,' said Olivia.

She brought her other hand out of her pocket, with more of the tansy dust, and went to blow it in Penny's face. But I moved forward quickly and blew it back into hers. She cried out once, then collapsed into Albert's arms. The impact knocked him to the floor and he sat there, holding his dying wife in his arms. Until she stopped breathing.

'You should have stuck with your original plan,' I said. 'And then we could all have had a nice pleasant evening together. Why did you change your minds and decide you'd rather murder your friends?'

Albert looked up and smiled slowly. 'It was the Voices. The Voices told us to do it.'

He leant over and kissed his dead wife on the lips, and the dust he took from her mouth was enough to kill him too.

Penny looked at me. 'Didn't you just know he was going to say that?'

# EIGHT
## Clean-up

I found my phone in a bag, along with all the other phones and the car keys, hidden in one of the wall hollows. I called the Colonel, and after a minimum of questions he called a cleaning crew. A local team turned up within the hour. At least, I assume they were local. I didn't see how they could have got there that quickly if they weren't. Quiet, professional young men and women, they pulled on hazmat suits and brought out the dead in body bags, then spent a really long time making sure no trace remained of anything that had happened at the Castle. No evidence, no clues, not even a speck of DNA. When the Organization cleans up, it does a thorough job. The everyday world can't be allowed to know about the kind of things we take for granted. And they definitely can't be allowed to know about me.

I didn't know what would happen to the bodies. I've never asked. I'm pretty sure I don't want to know.

'So the Castle will have a new legend,' said Penny, as we stood together out in the car park watching the cleaning crew pack up. 'Six people gathered here for a special meal, the Calverts and their old friends, and none of them were ever seen or heard of again.'

'Maybe Olivia was right,' I said. 'Nothing good has ever come out of the Castle.'

'And no one will ever know we were here.'

'Officially, we weren't. Only Olivia and Albert knew you'd been invited.'

Penny looked at me. 'What do you think Albert meant at the end? When he said the Voices made them do it?'

'I don't think he meant anything,' I said. 'He was just messing with our heads one last time. I wouldn't worry about it.'

Penny looked around the car park. All the cars had been

taken away apart from our hired car, which was standing beside the cleaners' anonymous white van. It was morning now, and a sour grey light fell heavily across the empty space.

'No hanging tree, no ghosts,' said Penny. 'All the old stories were just stories, after all.'

'Sometimes, that's how it works out,' I said.

'No demon, no alien.'

'No. Just a couple of very ordinary monsters.'

'Let's go home,' said Penny. 'These quiet evenings away will be the death of me.'